Syr Shaaow

Gordon Clark

Prologue

14th February 2005, Beirut, Lebanon

The parliamentary session had dragged on. Too many people attempting to make a name for themselves rather than talk about proposals for scheduling Lebanon's upcoming national elections. Not that Rafik Hariri was surprised by this: he too had been a new boy once, and to climb the great political ladder took time, effort and no small amount of getting yourself noticed. He sighed as the debate went a further time around the same circuit and looked down at his watch: he could think of plenty of other things he needed to do today. Things that would still be waiting for him when this session of posturing was over.

He ran a hand through his rapidly greying black hair, then brushed his grey moustache into some semblance of order. His thick black eyebrows came next as he rubbed his forehead, the movement causing his loose jowls to lift slightly.

Where did my youth go? he wondered absently.

Born in the Southern Lebanese port city of Sidon, Rafik had left home and moved to Saudi Arabia to seek his fortune in the oil-rich land. He'd started working there as a teacher, then moved into accountancy, before finally making it in the building trade. It paid to be flexible, he thought. With a mixture of luck and hard work he won a project, in 1977, to build the Saudi Taif Massara Hotel, a project he completed well ahead of time. The hotel was backed by the Saudi Crown Prince, and Rafik suddenly had a Royal Approval to his name and was granted Saudi citizenship. The rest, as they say, is history.

Returning to Lebanon a multi-millionaire, Rafik had used the skills he'd learned in Saudi to help rebuild his country. It was a country with a mess of forces all competing to control it — religion was split mainly between Muslims and Christians, but they also had their own internal divisions. Israel and Hezbollah traded rockets and raids down the years, taking turns to be the more successful and hold Lebanese territory and constant battles with President Assad for dominance in the control of politics led to Syrian troops occupying parts of the country.

Rafik often wondered if he should sell up and move to Paris, where his good friend President Jacques Chirac had often suggested he should set-up home.

He had stayed on though, serving five terms as the Prime Minister of his country, finally resigning when the Syrians lobbied the parliament into allowing the President of Lebanon Emile Lahoud another term in office. Rafik's resignation had been accepted in October, barely four months previously and, since then, he had often wondered whether the invitation to Paris still stood.

Sometimes it is just better to leave than to fight on.

Lebanon needed to stand on its own feet and run its affairs without the influence of outsiders such as Assad of Syria. They needed to make peace with their neighbours and reconstruct the battered infrastructure of the country. Rafik assisted in this with building programmes, but this was just touching the tip of the iceberg.

There was plenty of work left to do, and he wasn't one to run away from a fight, even though he was a little more worried recently at how personal and tense things were getting. It wasn't an emotion that he allowed to surface though.

He suddenly noticed that the people around him were clapping and the session was in closure. He'd probably missed the whole of the last ten minutes of discussions as he drifted through the years of his life. Not that it mattered; he would run through the whole thing again in his car with his good friend Basil Fuleihan, his former Minister for the Economy, weighing up the pros and cons. That interchange would also drift around various other topics until it finally drew to a close somewhere around midnight with a fine French cognac at his home. Possibly one he had been given by Jacques.

He stood to leave, shaking hands with friends and foes alike, always a professional politician. Basil was a few seats up from him, and as he caught up with him, he took his arm and leaned close. "I missed the final part," he told him.

"Me too. It was the most boring session I remember this year."

They exchanged a wry smile. "So no point asking you to ride with me and fill the gaps," Rafik asked.

"No, but I can still join you at your place for drink or two later."

They moved towards the door and outside into the bright Mediterranean sunlight. Rafik stopped, turning his face to the warm rays, a soft breeze cooling the sun nicely. "It's so good to be home. I may have made my money in Saudi, but the heat there was often unbearable. This is like heaven."

Basil grinned and poked his friend in the stomach. "Stop feeling sorry for yourself! It must be hell to be a billionaire."

Rafik tried to look hurt. "So you don't ride with me?"

"I need to have a few words with Ramy, but we'll meet up again later."

The two men started towards the line of cars, their own people lined up in a minor motorcade of 4 x 4 vehicles, all bullet-proofed. There had been a number of attempted assassinations in recent months, mainly aimed at people who opposed the Syrian influence in the country, so Hariri had decided to use some of his wealth to ensure the security of his support staff.

He again stopped and stood in the sun, watching as people exited the parliament and came down the steps towards their own line of vehicles. Everyone was smiling and talking, and not for the first time he wondered how the country, so divided, could appear to be so at peace.

He climbed into the rear of his car and spoke a few words to the driver. The rest of the team also mounted up and it was time to go.

"Let's go down by the port and then on towards home around the coast," he said. "Should look nice with the sun setting over the ocean."

"Yes Sir!" the man replied. "I'll take it nice and slow as you like it."

"Good man."

He looked back at the Lebanese Parliament building, its light sandstone bright in the low sun, its two levels of windows dark in shadows, and the tall arched door inviting those who wanted to become involved in the politics of the land. He thought about how many hours he had spent in there trying to figure out ways to better his country: to take control of the destiny of the place and free it from outside forces: his calls to world leaders, especially to King Fahd of Saudi Arabia whom, along with Chirac, he counted as a close friend.

The driver pulled away and the car glided towards Majidive, an area next to the international port. He could see large container vessels and massive cranes cutting up the blue sky, swaying left and right with the cargoes that kept a nation alive.

The motorcade turned to the left, away from the port, moving at a steady thirty miles an hour towards the Yacht Club Marina. Grand yachts — mainly large white, sleek-looking creatures — stood at the quayside, a sure indication of the wealth that the area boasted despite the troubles and divisions in Beirut. Farik was tempted to call a stop and go down to the waterside cafes and restaurants, to take a glass of cold white wine and perhaps some calamari. Even as Prime Minister he had done this sort of thing. It had kept him as 'one of us' in the people's eyes. A normal person.

He looked ahead at the St George Hotel, thinking it could also be a good choice of venue.

Travelling along the Wafik Sinno, looking out at the boats and dreaming, he did not register any of the events that happened in the next seconds: events that ended his life with a smile on his face as he imagined the first mouthful of cold white wine slipping over his lips.

Reports as to exactly what happened varied hugely. Some said a massive lorry rammed into the motorcade, its deadly cargo of explosive weighing up to two and a half tonnes. Some said it was a roadside device, a car bomb. Some, an aerial hit from the Israelis. No-one was sure, and in the end, it didn't really matter.

The explosion broke windows more than a mile away from its epicentre, took building facades clean away, and left a crater, more than fifteen feet wide, in the street. Cars were thrown from where they were parked onto the sidewalk and through shop windows, some of them blazing. Trees were felled. Civilians had no chance, and nor did the majority of the motorcade.

Rafik Hariri's 4 x 4 was destroyed and his life ended there. The death count eventually settled on twenty-one, with more than a hundred others injured or maimed.

Hariri was buried with his loyal bodyguards and staff close to the Mohammad Al-Amin Mosque, and a monument was erected by the road at the site of the explosion.

It was a very sad day for the country of Lebanon.

Chapter One

14th June 2011, Damascus, Syria

The morning air was crisp, a slight breeze making it chilly to the naked skin, but soon the temperature would increase, the sun already up in the early blue sky. Ahmed pulled the sheet over his young head and tried to hold onto the bed's warmth, not interested in getting up for another day at school. The wish to stay warm and lazy lasted only about another five minutes until his mother's voice broke the silence for a second time that morning.

"Ahmed, you'll be late for school! Come and get your breakfast now!"

Reluctantly he rolled out of bed and grabbed a half-clean T-shirt from the tidy pile of clothes on his chair. Mum had been sorting out the usual heap he had left the night before. He smiled.

At twelve years of age, he was a tall boy, already standing about five feet three. His thick mess of black hair lived in a constant tangle except for the three days a week that mum insisted it was washed, then it hung in soft curls down to his neck for that day, before becoming a tangle again once he retired to bed.

He pulled on a pair of jeans and training shoes and went into the bathroom. A splash-wash and a quick scrub of the teeth, and he was ready to face the day.

He bounded down a flight of stairs into the kitchen where his mother had a pile of fruit and vegetables waiting for him. A basket of breads sat in the centre of the table.

"Don't rush it down!" she told him.

He ignored her, wolfing down some bread and a couple of tomatoes, dipping the bread into some hummus, then grabbing an apple and banana before leaving the table.

"See you tonight mum," he called after him, grabbing the school bag on the way out.

His mother frowned, adjusting her veil as she prepared to leave the house. Kids.

In the street in front of their apartment he met a couple of his friends from school. Pushing and teasing one another as kids do, they headed off in to the streets of Damascus to walk the mile and a half that took them to their classroom. Along the way, others joined.

Walid, one of the kids from a better-off family, reached into the undergrowth between buildings and picked up a stick, held it to his shoulder and made explosive sounds.

"Did you see the stuff on Sky TV?" he asked them. "Soldiers shooting everyone all over the place in Aleppo."

The others looked at one another, a little nonplussed, but nodded that yes, it had looked amazing. Most did not have the privileges of Walid, especially the luxury of Sky in their homes.

"The television said that the President is going to get rid of all the terrorists and rebels out there that are threatening our safety," Walid went on. "He'll carry on protecting us from the bad guys, just like Superman."

Now he was talking about someone the others knew. Interest sparked.

"How does he do this?" asked Ahmed.

"He gets the army to shoot all the bad guys." The stick-gun was back in to the shoulder and he aimed at some of the girls along the street. "We can start by getting rid of the witches up front."

A couple of the other lads found their own sticks. Ahmed frowned: he was starting to notice girls in a different way recently, but anyway found an odd-shaped branch and gave in to peer pressure. After shooting the girls, they patrolled their way to the playground, guided in the intricacies of this art by the television-sage Walid.

Saumaya fascinated Ahmed. She was also twelve years of age, but years ahead of the other girls, both intellectually and in her physical development. She was starting to develop bumps and curves in places that he had never seen on anyone except the older ladies: the other girls in his class had none or almost none.

When he spoke to her, he found he couldn't look into her eyes for more than a few seconds. He just blushed if he did, so he always had to find an excuse to turn his head: he would talk to someone else, or show her a bird in a bush, or a picture in a book: Anything to escape those dark, deep, mysterious orbs that seemed to be able to read his mind.

Lost in his own thoughts, he totally missed the fact that she was coming over to his desk in a break between lessons.

"Hi Ahmed," she said, smiling at him. He wondered if she sensed his embarrassment, the smile seeming to taunt him. "Would you walk home with me after school. I want to talk about the maths lesson today." Everyone knew Ahmed was the best in the class at mathematics, so this was a reasonable request, but he still felt horribly uncomfortable. Want would the others think if he walked home alone with Saumaya?

"I, ummm, I think I promised Walid to play soldiers with him today."

"Play soldiers, or assist me with maths? What is more important?"

7

He looked down at his feet, the eyes had got to him again, he could feel the colour rising in his cheeks. What to say?

"Of course the maths is important. But Walid is my friend."

"And what am I Ahmed?" she challenged.

"Of course you are also a friend. But you are a girl." He knew it sounded pathetic as he said it, but it was out now.

"I thought you were growing up Ahmed, not like the bunch of idiots that surround Walid." He looked at her, surprised by the anger in her voice and the insult to his friends. Their eyes met, hers wild and challenging, his trying to find an avenue of escape.

"I'm sorry Saumaya," he managed.

"So do you walk me home or not?"

At three o'clock the school bell sounded the end of another day of studies. The classrooms drained of students quickly: corridors filled then emptied, and groups of like-minded children grouped and gossiped out in the play yard. They separated by classes and age groups at this age, rather than the religious and political divides that would later shape their lives.

"Hey Ahmed, you coming patrolling?" Walid shouted. "We have ten already to check the streets on the way home. Should be fun."

"Not today," Ahmed said. "Tomorrow. On the way to school."

"What have you got to do today?" Walid was puzzled. What was better than playing soldiers of the famous President Assad?

"Other stuff," Ahmed told him evasively.

"Like what exactly?"

Ahmed's mind raced. Lie and get caught out, or just give a feasible excuse?

"I have to do a bit of extra maths tuition with Saumaya," he replied. True, but not too true.

"Playing with girls? Hey guys, Ahmed is playing with the girls."

"It's maths tuition," Ahmed countered, but the other boys were in full flow now.

"Ahmed plays with the girls!"

They left on their patrol, rifle-sticks at the ready.

Damascus is one of the oldest continuously inhabited cities in the world and has changed hands often during its long history. It has seen the Crusaders, the Romans and the growth of Islam during its time, and the buildings around the city bear testimony to this. Sitting on the Barada River, the centre is dominated by the Umayyad Mosque, built on the site of St John's Church, but the Roman influence can also be seen in the Jupiter Temple at the entrance of Al-Hamidiyah Souq.

It is a sprawling city of around two million people, the centre high-rise, but this dropping away to normal housing as it spreads out in every direction, covering an area of almost forty square miles.

Both Ahmed and Saumaya lived in the north-west of the city and in sight of the Presidential Palace. As they left the Sami Aldroubi High School, the girl stopped.

"You were brave today Ahmed. Most boys would have simply agreed to go with Walid."

Ahmed's cheeks coloured, something that seemed to happen more and more as he spent time with Saumaya.

"It was nothing. I told you I would help you, so here I am."

They began walking north towards the area of Al Mouhajrin, silent but very aware of one another's presence. Ahmed broke the quiet.

"What can I help you with?" he asked. "What is the maths problem?"

Saumaya smiled. "No real problem, but if you could explain the geometry thing we did today, I'm sure it would be much clearer for me."

"The Pythagoras thing?"

"Yes," she responded. "And I just like talking to you too. Much better than with my girlfriends."

Ahmed looked towards her, only to find her big brown eyes already fixed on his, a smile on her lips. It was time to go red again.

Later, on the walk they saw some of the boys with Walid, stalking along people's garden walls, popping around corners and shooting each other. Ahmed looked at Saumaya who was already grinning and he found himself doing the same. He didn't blush.

"You're getting used to me," she told him.

He hesitated. "I guess I am."

"I like you Ahmed. You're not stupid like the rest of the oafs in the class."

"Thanks. You are also different from the other girls. More... adult, I think is the word."

"Thank you too."

They walked on, getting more comfortable. "Would you like to be my boyfriend Ahmed?"

"It would be my honour Saumaya."

She took his hand. Life was simple and great. 'If only it could have stayed this way' he would think in later times.

Chapter Two

3rd January 2013, Beirut, Lebanon

Jack Kearney looked out of his hotel room window and had to admit to himself once again the view was spectacular. Looking slightly to his left, he had the blue and white speckled Mediterranean Sea, the odd luxury yacht making its way slowly through a minute swell. Looking up and moving to his right, he had a clear blue sky without a cloud in sight.

He switched his gaze further to his left, raising his eyes. Mountains towered straight from the coast, green and rocky. He was told you could even ski on them in the winter months, then come down and swim in the Med on the afternoon. Heaven.

His eyes continued their downward path and finally reached the sprawl of tower blocks that ran from halfway up the hills down to the old town of Beirut and then to the sea. A panoramic view if ever there was one.

'What went wrong here?' he murmured to himself.

Beirut was a city of great seafood, good wines and friendly people. Every woman he remembered seeing there was glorious — dark hair and darker eyes to match, curves in all the right places, and a dress sense to be applauded anywhere on the planet. The architecture, though it was often damaged by the years of conflict, was beautiful and with a strong influence of old Southern France. If you half closed your eyes and took out the dirty and bomb-damaged walls, you could easily be in Nice or Marseille.

He released his breath and took and had another sip of the coffee he'd made in his room. That would be his breakfast this morning, but lunch would probably come out of a mess-hall in the barracks area, his men operated from, close to the airport. After five months this was really a routine, but he wondered if he'd miss it when his United Nations tour of the country was over in twenty-eight days' time. It had been a quick five months and all the talk in the unit was about a return to home. To Ireland and the other countries that were home for the motley crew that was his team. But somewhere in his heart he knew he'd be back.

He was a Major in the UK's Royal Irish Regiment, but attached to the United Nations Peace Keeping Force (UNIFIL) in Lebanon. It wasn't a usual detachment for his unit, but friends of his in the Irish Army had assisted him in getting a secondment 'to gain experience.' He had been in the RIR for eight years and, at twenty-seven years of age, a little young for his seniority. His time had earned him service in Afghanistan and Iraq, the former while the conflict there had raged and the latter in the aftermath of the second Gulf War. He had medals for both roles, plus a Military Medal for actions in Kabul that had probably saved five men's lives and cost him a month in hospital with a bullet in his chest.

Without being consciously aware of it, he rubbed the area with his left hand, his right again lifting the coffee cup and draining the dregs. Time to go.

Picking his pale blue beret off the television cabinet, he turned to the mirror. At six foot one inch tall, he was a fairly large man and this certainly helped when trying to assert his authority over others, whether they be from the military or not. He wore desert boots and light-coloured disruptive-pattern combat trousers over his long legs, while a green T-shirt covered his well-muscled upper body. The words 'Green Machine' were emblazoned across the chest. His dark hair was cut to a number two length — not US Marine style buzz cut, just bloody short. It made it quicker to wash and no time to comb.

He adjusted his beret; the left-hand-side tight on his scalp and the right pulled down slightly over his ear. The unit crest was somewhere between his left eye and left ear. He knew as a Major he should try and look more 'uniform' but he still favoured the jaunty image he had adopted as a young soldier. Somehow staying within the military law but pushing it to the outer boundaries.

He lifted the lightweight combat jacket off the bed and covered the T-shirt, then picked up and shouldered a small backpack with the documents that should get him through the day and switched off the television. Final glance around the room and off to the door.

Three minutes later he was in a minibus on his way to work.

The Irish Army formed a part of the United Nations Peacekeeping Force in Lebanon (UNIFIL) since the late 1970s, with around 30,000 Irish soldiers spending time in the country over a twenty-three year period. Their initial brief was to supervise the withdrawal of the Israeli Defence Force following the invasion of Lebanon in 1978 by Israel, and to stop fighting between the Palestine Liberation Organisation and the Israeli military.

When Israel again invaded Lebanon in 1982, their role became even more difficult as they tried to control and monitor guerrilla warfare between the Israelis, the South Lebanon Army, and the Hezbollah. Forty-seven of their men died before their withdrawal from the region in 2001 following the Israeli exit from Southern Lebanon, after which only eleven Irish troops stayed there as UN observers.

In 2006 a couple of hundred were returned to the country to provide security for a unit of engineers from Finland. After a year, this operation was also complete and the Irish returned to their home.

The 104 Infantry Battalion has now been in Lebanon since 2011 on monitoring and observation duties.

Jack entered his offices and nodded to the Corporal on the front desk.

"Anything new overnight Corps?" he asked.

"Not really Sir. Couple of shots reported close to the border by Deir El Aachayer, but no kidnapping reports or troop movements."

"Great. That's close to Damascus isn't it?" He received a nod. "Is the coffee fresh?"

"Made it about an hour back."

"Perfect," he said, grabbing a mug from the draining board.

He poured a good measure of black coffee and headed through to his own small office. It was bare of clutter — a desk, chair, filing cabinet and a cupboard where he left his deployment clothing, webbing and sports clothing. On one wall was a large scale map of Lebanon showing flags, where troops were and incidents had occurred, in various coded colours; another wall with a white board with notes on it; the third wall with the door he'd entered and finally a window looking out on a parking area. Nothing too exciting.

Moving to the map, he looked along the border with Syria, thinking that once upon a time his focus would have been further south with the Israeli border. At present, this was fairly quiet, but the troubles over the eastern frontier more than compensated for this.

Since the initial uprising in the Syria during the Arab Spring, the internal conflict there had become an all-out civil war that posed a real danger of spilling over into neighbouring countries, especially Lebanon. Already refugees were flooding over the border, with an estimated 350,000 in the border areas. Apart from assisting the Lebanese Army with security and their observation role in the country, the Irish Army were now also caught-up in the distribution and protection of humanitarian aid.

And the camps — some larger than the local towns — were already stretched to breaking point, both on the Lebanese and the Syrian sides of the border. Jack knew that things were getting especially bad in the Beddawi Refugee Camp in the north, but also heard of problems across the border in Yarmouk, where the Syrian authorities sometimes stopped the aid workers from accessing the homeless people.

Jack had read a report only days before, from Oxfam, estimating that seven million people within Syria required humanitarian aid. Perhaps the report was slanted towards drumming-up donations, but even if the figure was only fifty million this had serious implications for all of the surrounding countries. And it was fine to house people in tented accommodation during the summer months, but what could they look forward to during a harsh winter?

He moved to his desk and looked at the new print-outs neatly stacked in his in-tray. As Corporal McCarthy had told him, no new hostage reports, but a few incidents of trouble within the camps themselves. Fights at crowded water stations, theft of food and clothing, a beating for a man who had looked too long at a woman trying to feed her baby... All things that can and will happen when too many people are forced to

13

survive together in a cramped and crowded place. It didn't make it any better, but this would happen anywhere in the world under the same circumstances.

He sipped on his coffee, the thought passing through his mind that maybe the one he'd made himself in his room that morning had tasted better.

"Anything I need to know about for today?" he called through to McCarthy. The man came into his office with a pad.

"A couple of convoys up to the border with food aid, but we've got Captains O'Leary and Clarke on those, so nothing for you Sir." He looked down the list a little further. "There're some new lads arriving in from Dublin today who'll need an intro, then a bit of training before we let them loose on the ladies here," he joked. "Oh, and an American politician visiting the camp for lunch. You want to meet him?"

"No, let's leave the CO to handle that," Jack said. "I'll join one of the convoys."

"One's leaving at eleven to the area the shots were reported last night. Camp just over the border. Should be back about six this evening."

"I'll join that one."

The Corporal checked a second page of his file. "That one will be with Captain Clarke," he told Jack. "You want me to tell him you'll be joining?"

"No Corps, I'll call him myself. Cheers!"

The convoy was made up of five civilian articulated lorries. Only ten soldiers, split between two Land Rovers, travelled with them, more of a token than a deterrent for a determined attacker, but it gave at least a little comfort to the civilian lorry drivers who knew no better.

They assembled at the edge of Beirut on a large area of rough ground.

"Has everyone got enough water with them?" The drivers were being asked by Tim Clarke, the twenty-three year old Captain running the show. "Something to eat? Make sure you keep anything worth having hidden — these people are desperate and will take anything on offer."

A local translated everything into Arabic, though most people in Lebanon understood a good deal of English. Tim watched and waited.

The convoy followed the main road out to Zahle and up into the hills and mountains surrounding the city. Soon they passed the town of Aley, then climbed more to Hammana and Chtaura. Here they branched off to the right, heading towards the border and Masnaa. If they kept rolling on this road they would eventually reach Damascus. Before that, the border would stop them though.

It was mountainous up here and the lorries laboured on some of the gradients. During the winter months the place was deep in snow, and during more peaceful times the queues of trucks waiting to cross sometimes stretched for miles. Now almost nothing was permitted to cross, so there were no lines of traffic to hold them up.

The gated area that was the official crossing point loomed in the distance. Between where they were and the border post, military patrols roamed randomly, but if you really wanted to cross from one side to the other it was quite easy, especially under cover of darkness. Illegal goods came and went freely during the night, neither side trying too hard to stop the trade. In truth, the same soldiers patrolling the frontier were often involved in the work.

Two hundred yards short of the gate, Tim pulled the convoy over.

"We have to leave you on your own from here," he told the drivers, who were stretching their legs and having a smoke. "The camp isn't far, so we'll just hang around for an hour or two until you return. I'll move up to the gate with the paperwork and get things ready for you. Coming?" Tim asked, turning to Jack. Why not? he thought, picking up his SA 80 rifle and marching with Tim towards the offices by the gate.

Hanging the weapon over his left shoulder he looked ahead to see a group of armed men by the office door. They looked like civilians, but the Kalashnikovs hanging on their arms, though old, looked deadly enough to be taken seriously. As he got closer he also noted that their ages ranged from about fifteen to forty. He counted fourteen of them.

"Looks a bit like a reception committee," said Tim.

"You know how much they love you Irish."

Ignoring the group, the two soldiers walked towards the door. A couple of the men got up, the older of them moving towards them.

"Stop soldiers," he said. "You do not need to go in there. We are here from the Free Syrian Army to escort the convoy to the camp. You can leave now."

Tim turned to him slowly. "And who might you be Sir?" he asked politely. "I was led to believe the Syrian escort would wait on the far side of the border."

"What is a border friend?" the man asked smiling.

"Do you have some ID?"

"Nothing you need to see."

"Then I'm afraid we will return to Beirut with the supplies."

A tense silence ensued. Both men looked into each other's eyes, not daring to give an inch. Another couple of the men stood, nervously picking up their guns.

Jack stepped forward. "I think you are aware of the rules Mister No-name. We will not surrender the convoy to you without the correct paperwork, so no point continuing this discussion. Captain Clarke and myself will be off now."

He steeled himself for a burst of action, wishing his rifle was on his right arm and not his left and trying to show no fear or emotion. He felt the presence of Tim by his side but did not dare to look at him as it looked like weakness. He turned away from the men.

"English!" he heard from the nameless Syrian. "We are still talking to you. Stand still!"

Jack swung swiftly through ninety degrees until he faced the man again. He moved to within an inch of his face, eye to eye. He could smell the sweat from his dirty clothes and spices on his breath.

"First, dickhead, I am not English. And second, you don't ever tell me what to do. You may think you are a soldier, but actually you are probably a car mechanic, or a janitor. I am trained to eat people like you for fun."

He spun away, feeling their eyes on him. He waited to hear the cocking of a weapon, but no sound came. He heard the footfalls of Tim beside him.

"Quite a performance boss," Tim murmured. "Think we'll get away with it?"

Jack was calming down, breathing again. "Sure, we're on the Lebanese side of the border. And we're Irish." He grinned, but not so the rebels could see it.

"You're fucking mad!" Tim told him.

Ten minutes later the Syrians had moved out. Across the border they made a show of firing rounds into the air, whooping like kids. The Irish troops watched, unimpressed. Most of them had already seen service in Liberia and Chad and knew things could get much worse.

The two officers again moved up to the border post. This time they were met by customs officers and the paperwork was completed.

"Do you think the convoy will get past those guys?" Tim asked the senior of the officials.

"If you give them another ten minutes, I think so. Those guys were just looking for an easy hit. Now they're fed-up and heading home."

Two boring hours later the lorries returned empty. It was time to go home.

By the time they made camp at six-thirty in the evening, Jack's confrontation with the Free Syrian Army was barracks headline news. The CO was soon over as they handed in their weapons at the armoury.

"Hear you've been bullying the locals again Jack," he said. "Scared them shitless?"

"They did a fair job of worrying me too Sir. Wasn't all one sided."

"Not the version I heard."

Jack grinned and returned to his office. The CO watched him go, wishing the Major wasn't just on detachment to him. He'd make a damned fine colonel one day.

By seven, Jack had finished all he needed to do and called the Duty Driver. He shared a lift down the hill to the hotel with Tim Clarke and John McCarthy from the second convoy escort and they agreed to meet for dinner after a beer or two. Eight o'clock at the bar.

But first a shower and a shave. He could still smell the rebel leader's breath and sweaty clothing.

Chapter Three

10th January 2013, Damascus, Syria

The beautiful city of Damascus was being systematically destroyed, road by road, brick by brick. Buildings hundreds of years old yielded to the power of tank shells and rockets, heavy artillery and mortars. Houses were pockmarked with bullet wounds, black smoke scarred a skyline backed by snow topped hills and the smell of death oozed out of everywhere. Cars lay crushed by tank tracks.

The sickness in Syria had finally reached the capital.

Businesses tried to function as usual, but with most the rest of the world refusing to trade with you, this was an impossible feat.

The whole country was in meltdown.

Problems had spread to Syria as they did to the majority of Middle Eastern countries in early 2011 on the back of the so-called 'Arab Spring.' In Syria, the demonstrators called for the standing down of Syria's President, Bashar al-Assad, and an end to the Ba'ath Party. The Assad family had ruled the country since 1971.

The Ba'ath party came to power in Syria in 1964, with the Assad clan gaining power in 1970 through General Hafez al-Assad. He appointed himself Prime Minister in 1971 and held the post until his death in 2000, when his son Bashar was given the position at the age of thirty-four, this after amending the constitution to allow such a young leader.

From the moment the Ba'ath Party took power, emergency rule was introduced in the country, allowing police and troops to imprison and hold individuals as they wished. Their excuse was that Syria was constantly at war with neighbouring Israel. Protestors and activists were held without charge and tortured, often in jail conditions not acceptable to humans anywhere else on the planet.

And so on to the Arab Spring. In April of 2011 during crowd gatherings in several towns and cities, Syrian Army soldiers fired on civilian demonstrators. The government labelled them as 'armed terrorists and foreign mercenaries.' Not even the Arab League believed this, and along with Europe and America condemned the use of force against civilians, eventually suspending the country's membership from the League.

Soldiers began leaving their units and, along with civilians, started forming organised opposition groups. They were small groups at first, but as time went by links formed between the various groups and the Free Syrian Army came into being.

Daraa, a city in the south of the country, became known as 'The Cradle of the Revolution' when crowds clashed with police in March 2011, resulting in several deaths. A few days later the Ba'ath headquarters in the city was burned to the ground. In the following two days the police shot and killed fifteen protestors.

Sparked by this, further crowds gathered in on the Friday 18th March, to be known as the 'Friday of Dignity'. They demanded, amongst other things, an end to almost fifty years of emergency powers. The protests spread on quite a large scale countrywide, including Damascus, al-Hasakah, Daraa, Hama and Banias.

After prayers the following Friday, over 100,000 people paraded in Daraa. Twenty of them were killed.

Security forces began a campaign of arresting and detaining anyone suspected of being an activist or human rights campaigner, subjecting them to torture, electric shocks and beatings. The law was altered to allow them to hold 'suspects' for eight days without a warrant. Communities not aligned to the President received particular attention.

At the end of April, Assad conceded to some of the popular demands, including the end to emergency powers and promised salary increases and job opportunities. Many never came to pass.

Saumaya was fourteen now, as was Ahmed. They were still young, but in their society people of this age often needed to work in adult jobs and take on the life of someone way beyond their years. War had been a part of their young lives on and off for almost two years now. They had seen things that most adults in the 'normal world' would never experience, and probably hoped they would never have cause to.

Ahmed's father had been taken away late one night by one of the states eighteen security establishments. Ahmed didn't know which one: he also didn't know if he'd ever come back. That had been eight months previous, after a series of confrontations between the President's men and the rebels. Many people didn't come back. Elacha — Ahmed's mother — resigned herself to this after the third month of absence.

Saumaya had lost both of her parents during a shelling by government forces on the area they had lived in. Rebel forces were supposedly hiding out there, so a bombardment of civilian accommodation followed. They were unlucky enough to be home at the time.

What was left of the family — Saumaya and her ten year old brother — was left to fend for itself, but Ahmed had mentioned this to his mother and she had insisted they came to live with them. His mother was aware that Saumaya and he were together, but she didn't mind this. In normal circumstances she would not have wished for a better daughter-in-law. As things were, it sort of gave her and them a family again, slightly filling the gap left by her man.

So far, their house had been spared in the fighting, but in the Syria of today, it was uncertain as to how long this luck could last. Many of their friends had lost their homes and moved in with other family members or good neighbours. Others had taken the big step and fled their country, but the tales that drifted back from the refugee camps in Lebanon, Turkey, Jordan and Iran meant people really viewed this as a last resort.

After one of the battles between government and rebel forces, Ahmed had found himself a gun but had stayed out of the fighting. After his father had been taken, he wanted to join the rebels, but his mother had pleaded with him not to. He saw the weapon as a way to protect his family from more upsets and despite getting stick about being a coward from the local men, he had honoured his mother's wishes. For now.

There was no school now. No teachers, so no school. Most of the teachers had fled across the border to look for work, and others had joined the Free Syrian Army in the hope of returning their country to peace.

Saumaya and Ahmed tried to teach the younger children. With his natural leaning to mathematics, he was able to educate them to a reasonable level. He also had the text books for the work he was missing now, and with his appetite for the subject he was actually getting ahead of the syllabus — if one had existed. Saumaya taught religion and language, so between them an education of the local youth continued. This 'community service' helped to pacify the men that wanted Ahmed to join the fighters and had less honourable intentions for the young Saumaya.

It was an uneasy peace.

Sitting under the shade of a large olive tree in Tishreen Park in the Al-Malki district of Damascus, it was easy to forget that the region was experiencing a civil war. The Barada River flowed nearby, and the long grass hid the young lovers from the view of prying eyes while the trees cooled the sunlight. It was place where families had Friday picnics in peaceful times, but now somewhere almost no-one went to.

"Why is our country in such a mess?" Saumaya asked Ahmed. "We have such a beautiful land, but we seem determined to ruin it."

Ahmed rolled off his back to look at her. "It will get better again one day."

She also rolled over towards him, her hand releasing his and moving to his face. He put a hand on her waist and drew her to him. They kissed.

"I love you Saumaya."

"And I love you Ahmed. We will always be together."

The kiss was longer this time, and his hand slipped over her breast. Her breathing became a little faster and her tongue slipped into his mouth. He rolled her on top of him and his other hand felt her behind through her dress. She pushed herself up, looking down at him.

"I want to do it Ahmed, but I think it is the wrong place and time."

"I will not rush you Saumaya. We are getting close to fifteen, but we have all of our lives for this. There is no rush."

She lowered her body back beside his, her head on his shoulder. "Thank you Ahmed," she breathed onto his olive skin.

They kicked the door in at three o'clock in the morning. Everyone in the house was asleep, but the sound of a heavy boot splitting the wooden frame, followed immediately by loud and angry voices woke everyone in the place.

Boots thudded through the house, some climbing the stairs. Ahmed rolled out of bed, a little confused from the fast transition from sleep, wishing he hadn't hidden the weapon outside in the yard. Suddenly his mind snapped fully into life, his own danger forgotten as he thought of Saumaya and his mother, knowing the women were the most in danger. He pulled on a pair of jeans and opened the bedroom door as the first soldiers reached the top of the stairs.

"Get back in your room now!" he was ordered. He saw his mother in a nightdress opening her door and headed straight towards her.

"I said your room!" the soldier yelled at him. "Right now!"

He continued towards his mother, then saw Saumaya leaving her room too.

"What do you want?" he challenged the soldiers. "You've taken my father already." He hoped the men would focus on him and not on the girls.

"Get back to your room kid."

"But I have to look after my family. These are women and children here!"

"Final warning: get to your room!"

He carried on towards his mother and girlfriend. Suddenly a rifle butt smashed into the back of his head and he was out cold.

He came to about thirty minutes later. He was in his room with his hands and ankles tied. His head was swimming. He tried to lie still to stop the pain, and then he heard noises from the other rooms.

"Stop it you bastards!" he cried as loud as he could, trying to free himself. "Leave my family alone!"

He could hear whimpering from his mother's room. He knew what was happening even though he couldn't see it, could hear the springs of the bed creaking. He could also

21

hear Saumaya begging that the soldiers stopped raping his mother, asking them to please leave her alone. They just laughed and continued.

"It's your turn next bitch," one of them told her. "You shouldn't support the rebels."

The cries of the women, the harsh, laughing voices of the men, the smell gun oil all rushed through Ahmed's mind, paralyzing him for a few seconds. He needed to get free and now. He struggled with his bonds, blocking everything else, but to no avail.

"You bastards!" he cried out. "Come and fight me!"

The door of his room opened and a semi-naked soldier walked in. "Shut-up you bloody rebel. I should kill you now!"

"Fight me! Leave my family!"

"I said shut it!" Something hard hit him on the head again and he was once again unconscious.

The next time he awoke the house was dark and quiet. He felt his head stick to the pillow when he tried to lift it, blood drying on the bedding. He tried to move his arms again, but they were still tied, his feet still trussed.

"Saumaya? Mum?" His voice sounded pathetic, childish, without hope. No answer. He tried again.

He thought he could hear crying, very soft, but just audible. He called again, but no answer. Then he remembered Sauyama's younger brother.

"Mohamed?" he tried. "Mohamed it's me, Ahmed. Come to help me."

At first nothing happened, but after calling for him for ten minutes, he persuaded the boy to come through.

"Untie me please."

When he was free he hugged the boy and calmed him down.

"I hid under the bed when the soldiers came," the youth said. "I think they have killed Saumaya."

"Stay here."

Ahmed went through door towards his mother's room, dreading what he might see. Taking a deep breath he pushed open the bedroom door. The room was dark. "Stay where you are Mohamed," he called. He could hear flies buzzing at his intrusion. A smell of blood and urine. He pushed himself forward into the darkness, pulling back one of the curtains and looked around.

He threw-up, through the open window, ill from the scene before him.

Both women were naked, bits of torn night clothing lying on the floor of the room. Both had their throats cut — jagged, open wounds — blood all over the bed. From the bruising on his mother's body, it was clear she had been raped, but also clear the soldiers had beaten her: her eyes swollen and bloody, purple welts on her ribcage.

Sauyama had been a virgin, and the area of the bed where her legs still lay open and abused was a mess of blood. Her face was a death mask of agony.

He moaned in a pain he could not describe, collapsing to the floor of the room and clutching at his stomach as he dry retched. He knew he would have nightmares about what was in front of him for years to come, knew this was as bad as anything he would experience in his life.

There was no God, of that he was sure. The time for peace was over.

He crawled out of the room, desperate for the taste of fresh air.

When he first went to the men in the street and offered to join them, they laughed at him. When they heard what had happened in the house, they welcomed him. Many of them had equally horrible tales to tell. They helped him bury the bodies. They found somewhere for Mohamed to live.

They took Ahmed back to Tishreen Park. This time was not for love, but to teach him about his gun.

He learned it was a Kalashnikov AK47, a weapon of choice amongst many revolutionaries. It was a machinegun, not a precision weapon, but one used to spray a target, forgiving to the non-marksman. They taught him how to strip it, to assemble it, to take care of the gun. It was a weapon that would work for long periods without any maintenance he was informed, but it was better to keep it clean. It would be less likely to let him down then.

After two days of building and stripping the machinegun and pretending to aim and fire, they said he was ready. It was time to fire it for real, but once fired they had to get out of the area quickly, before troops investigated the shots.

The older men set-up a target about a hundred feet away, hoping he'd hit it first time to give him more confidence. They had him load thirty rounds.

"OK," they told him. "Give it a try."

He raised the butt to his shoulder as he'd been shown and then brought the gun up to site along the barrel and foresight. His right thumb flicked the safety catch off. Just the trigger to pull. He squeezed it gently.

The weapon leapt in his hands and he almost dropped it. The men laughed.

"Have another go."

His ears were ringing and he took a firmer grip on the AK47. He was ready for the shock this time and hit the ground in front of the target, stones flying off the deck.

"And again."

He breathed as they'd told him to in training and had another burst of rounds. These ones hit the target, not perfect, but certainly a hit.

"Keep going boy. Keep firing short bursts until the magazine is empty."

He fired again, getting more confident until the breach block fell on an empty chamber. He made the weapon safe.

"OK, let's go before the bastards get here."

They left the park and went back to a derelict building where they operated from. It looked like a wreck, but under the rubble was a cellar and this was his new home.

He cleaned his gun in silence and waited for the chance to use it on the government troops.

Chapter Four

26th March 2013, Aleppo, Syria

The locals had assembled a net over the Aleppo River near to a bridge to catch the bodies. It was a gruesome job, and in the first three months of the year they had pulled out almost one hundred and fifty of them, mainly with a single bullet to the head. Very few of them wore a uniform, meaning they were almost certainly suspected of being with the Free Syrian Army, or one of the other bands not agreeing with President Assad.

Most were men, but women and children were also hauled out. Government Forces would point out that the same children were part of the rebel forces, and that they were trying to kill them just as surely as their parents would.

The hospitals were working without medicine, electricity, running water. They had no stocks of blood or saline solutions, no morphine to make an operation more humane. There were almost no doctors or nurses and everyone had to help their friends and families with whatever they had.

Could things possibly get worse?

The district had been a poor one, not a rich estate loyal to the President. Because of this the tanks had gone through it and the buildings were wrecked. Flats looked like packs of cards, wall lying in heaps on walls, layers of floors and ceilings one on top of another. Some walls still stood upright, but even these had shell holes in, or marks where bullets had scarred them.

The Government patrol of twelve men moved silently amongst the rubble that had been a street. They were dressed in disruptive pattern combat uniform, all had the same webbing and weapons, totally unlike the rebels who wore a mishmash of clothing and took what weapons they could.

Rifles cocked and ready, safeties off, the patrol leader scanned the streets warily, occasionally calling a stop. They would all drop to their knees behind cover and examine their part of the area in all around defence.

And then forward again.

The tanks had been to this district three times now, so opposition was not really expected. No building could really be considered a house anymore, but all the soldiers knew from bitter experience that people survived, and those that did survive were dangerous. They also heard stories from Damascus, Homs and other cities of what could happen if they were caught alive.

They dropped to their knees again on the commander's signal. Ahead was a large open area. No sign of life, but not the sort of place a soldier liked to be. No cover.

Watching. For five minutes only watching for any sign of life, any sign that this could be a bad place to be. Nothing.

The leader waved them up and they moved forward. With hand signals he ordered them to space out more than previously, making it harder for a defender to hit them all at once. They walked swiftly, suspiciously surveying the hundred and fifty feet of open space with its piles of ex-buildings off to the sides. Hopefully, their next patrol would be in armoured cars. Their weapons followed where their eyes looked, ready to shoot.

It happened in the middle of the clearing — where else. Two sets of men appeared to their front, possibly twenty in each group. All were armed and all were firing. Some soldiers died instantly, but even in the hail of fire from forty guns, some seemed to live a charmed life, at least for a short while.

After what seemed like an age but what actually took only a few minutes, the rebel commander called a cease fire.

"Stop firing!"

The silence was intense. After all the shooting the smell of cordite filled the air. No birds chirped. The only sound was from the couple of soldiers not dead, but badly wounded.

"Let's go and finish them," the chief said.

They came forward, checking each soldier as they reached him, firing an extra bullet where needed.

The rebel commander got to the Lieutenant who had led the Syrian Army patrol. His leg was shattered at thigh level and it was clear from the amount of blood on the road he would soon bleed to death. But he was alive.

"You bastard!" the rebel said, kicking him in the side. The soldier didn't move or squeal, more dead than alive.

The leader took out a large bayonet. "If they can do it in Homs, we can do it here," he told the half-dead youth. His men gathered around him. He had a reputation for violence that scared his own men.

Bending down over the soldier, he plunged the bayonet into his stomach just below the sternum and ripped down. The soldier still could not scream, but he moaned and twitched. "Kill me please," he muttered, barely audible.

The rebel sliced viciously at the stomach region, opening it up.

"Get a picture," he told one of his people.

One of the men got out a mobile phone and moved the others away a little to let him in. They were pleased to have an excuse to back off.

The leader reached into the stomach cavity, the Lieutenant no longer with them. He grabbed a handful of intestine and pulled on it, the stuff coming out like grey smelly sausage. He pushed the bayonet in and up under the rib cage, searching but not finding the heart. He did get a lump of lung though and pulled this out to follow the gut.

"This is what we do to our enemies," he yelled. "We kill them and eat them!"

He stuffed a piece of bloody lung in to his mouth, bright red blood dribbling down his chin. Two of his men threw up at the sight, turning away to try and avoid being noticed.

His number two stepped forward, taking the lung off the leader and helping himself to a bite.

A boy of ten followed suit, his weapon hanging carelessly from his shoulder and almost in contact with the ground, only a child.

A couple of others did the same. Some were still vomiting.

Doctor El Hachem leant over the boy of seven looking first at his face and then at his leg. He would lose his right eye, no doubt about that, but could he save his right leg? Below the knee it was a mess, the tibia and fibula both sticking out of the flesh, the ends jagged. Skin, tendons and muscle kept his foot attached to the rest of the leg. He was deep in shock and feeling nothing at all at the moment, but this would wear off and soon he would be screaming.

He knew that people would normally faint or throw-up at the sight, but El Hachim had witnessed it too often in recent months.

Before the conflict he would have X-rayed the leg to decide how to try and position it. Even then there was fair chance the damaged leg would end up slightly shorter than the good one, giving the young guy a limp for the rest of his life. Problem today was he had an X-ray machine, but no electricity, so therefore the machine was just a useless lump of electronics.

"Fuck," he cursed, feeling useless. It was an emotion he experienced frequently nowadays.

He looked around at the 'operating theatre' he was to work in. The bed was a steel frame. Bedding and mattresses had gone long ago, stolen by soldiers who had to rough it. Blood stained the floors and walls, despite the best efforts of the nurses and staff to keep the place clean. With no cleaning fluids, disinfectants, bleaches, or anything else including water often enough, hygiene was pretty low on the agenda. Fixing broken bodies was all he could do now.

The boy whimpered. The pain was starting to come through. He had to get started.

He used his fingers to feel the bone beneath the break. What he felt he didn't like – everything down there was in pieces, sharp fragments of bone everywhere, shattered by a bullet. It had to come off.

He took a lump of wood from the side and gave it to the boy's father.

"This is going to hurt. Put it in his mouth. It will stop him biting into his lips. I need to move fast before the pain hits him."

"Can't you give him morphine?"

"I don't have any. I don't have anything. I'm sorry."

The man was crying freely. "He's my only son."

"Try and be strong for him. I have to remove the lower leg before the pain comes, and before it becomes infected. Hold him. Help him." He couldn't look at the father. He couldn't look at the son.

The doctor started on his gruesome task.

The tanks rolled forward. It was rumoured the rebels had rocket-propelled grenade launchers, — RPGs, as described nonchalantly by the press corps. 'The rebels are armed with AK47s and RPGs' they would report, as though the man in the street knew everything about them. A sign of the times was that many of them did.

A burnt-out car was at the side of the road and the lead tank commander thought it would be fun to drive over it, instructing the driver to do so. The old Russian armour rolled up to the wreck, then one track crawled up the blackened bonnet. For a second the T-72 pointed skywards, then as it edged forward, gravity got the better of it and it slammed on to the roof of the vehicle, flattening it.

The commander and crew laughed together over the intercom.

"One-one-delta. Movement up ahead in the slightly red-coloured building, third right." The message sounded in the lead tank commanders ear. He looked at the building, saw nothing, but decided to throw a few shells at it anyway. The place was already full of holes, so a few more?

The tank jerked as the shells spat out of the cannon. A wall fell in a massive cloud of dust. A cheer from the crew. They felt great, encircled by an armoured shell.

"Another old car coming up on the left commander," the gunner squawked over the intercom. "What do you think?"

"Let's do it again Sir," the driver egged on.

"You're the driver."

The man with the levers froze his left track and slewed the steel lump towards the car. "Here we go!"

The T-72 rolled steadily towards the old wreck, a Toyota Land Cruiser in its day, but burnt out sometime during the troubles. Its tyres were gone, with just the steel wire that made up their strength hanging onto the end of the axles.

"Hold tight!" the driver yelled.

The tank hit the bonnet and started to climb onto the shell of a car. Again the front-end pointed to the heavens, slowly tipping back towards planet earth. It lowered slowly this time on to the car roof, the weight pressing down on it as the tracks dragged the tank towards the rear of the vehicle.

BANG! A ball of bright orange flame about seventy feet wide hid the tank and the Toyota.

"Shit!" the commander of the following T-72 shouted. "Stop! Stop!"

His tank ground to a halt, the other four behind him doing the same. The fireball was turning to smaller flames and black oily smoke.

"Back-up! We may be in an ambush zone!"

The rearmost tank began reversing the others following suit. The ammo in the burning lead tank reached a critical point and rounds and shells started exploding inside it. No-one got out.

A line of smoke suddenly hurtled in from about three hundred feet away, the RPG round hitting the number two tank and destroying the track. The driver didn't know this at first and continued driving, throwing the track fully off the vehicle, causing the giant steel hulk to slew around on the one track that was left. Realising what was happening, the driver finally came off the gas. The other tanks didn't notice, so occupied with trying to get out of the kill zone.

"We've lost a track." The commander spoke into the radio. "Can't move out of here."

Another smoke trail came from the same place as the first and hit the tank on the turret, but the armour held up. The noise inside the steel coffin was deafening. Even the hardest and most experienced soldier was panicking.

"They're using us for target practice," the boss told anyone on the net who might listen. "Come and get us out of here."

But the other four tank commanders had just one thought: get out of there.

The driver lost his nerve. Opening the hatch, he started to haul himself out, looking for cover. The next RPG round hit the side of the tank close to where he was, and a scalding piece of shrapnel hit him in the mouth, smashing the insides of his skull to pieces. He rolled down the steel front of the T-72 and onto the ground.

The gunner decided it was time to go. Deafened after the three hits and believing the driver had already escaped, he climbed out of the top hatch, only to be cut-down by small arms fire.

The other tanks were now releasing rounds towards where the RPG launcher was believed to be, but the rebels had already taken flight. They showered the buildings and rubble, reversing further and further from the two wrecked machines and dead comrades.

The Free Syrian Army claimed another victory.

The commander stayed in his tank, curled in a ball on the floor. It was his first experience of an enemy returning fire and he didn't like it.

A throng of around a thousand people — mainly — had assembled outside of the university just off Fatih Sultan Mehamed Avenue. They were fed-up with the fighting, the murder, the rape, with not being able to lead normal lives. They knew that protesting at the best of times was dangerous in Aleppo, and that right now it was more than dangerous, so they did nothing to panic the security forces, merely stood there to make their point.

The military were there in force. Tanks stood at one end of the square, troops had check points at each road entering and exiting the area. But it was peaceful.

In one of the upstairs rooms in an apartment block overlooking all of this, a man was setting up a camera and lo-tech satellite link. He wasn't really a reporter, but he would have told anyone that asked that he was one, someone intent on showing the outside world what was happening in Syria.

"Is it working?" a second man asked.

"Give me a minute."

The 'reporter' fiddled some more with the camera, making a hole in the net curtain to just allow the lens to pass through it. From the outside it should be invisible. He played with aperture settings and light levels until the picture of the crowd outside was clear. He practised zooming the image in and out, panning over and around the mass of people. Happy with the camera set up, he switched to the transmission dish and completed a self-test function.

All as good as he could hope for.

"It's good," he told the other man. The man took out his cell phone and dialled a number.

"We're ready in here," he told someone. He clicked off, not letting anyone have time to monitor the call.

At three points in the area, things began to happen.

A team of two men opened a window about one hundred and fifty feet from where the tanks were standing idle at the end of the square. One had an RPG 7 grenade launcher. The other had two spare launchers ready to hand over when the first was spent.

The second and third teams of two had a sniper's rifle apiece. Each of the teams moved to their own windows, which were situated at either side of the square. They checked watches and waited for the signal they knew was coming.

All three phones rang twice and then died.

"The first rocket hits the tank, then we pick targets. When the third rocket is gone, so are we," one of the riflemen told his colleague.

Ten seconds later the smash of a rocket hitting a tank turret, hatch open and commander standing in it. He was dead instantly.

The four snipers then started engaging targets, each one a soldier of the Syrian Army, still frozen to the spot from the shock of the explosion. First volley, four hits, second shots, three more…

The crowd panicked, not knowing what direction to move in.

The soldiers also lost it, looking for the source of the shots and only seeing the crowd running at them, trying to get away from the danger. But to a young man with a gun, it looked like they were coming for them.

The second RPG round hit a soft-skinned command vehicle that immediately caught fire. More bullets took more soldiers. Another RPG round. Another hit and explosion.

The soldiers began firing indiscriminately in to the thousand-strong crowd.

By the time order was restored fifteen minutes later, over a hundred military and civilians were dead and treble that number wounded.

The pictures were on all major news channels within an hour. First with Al Jazeera whom the rebels leaked it to, but then with CNN, BBC, NBC and Fox.

Another massacre in Aleppo. Government forces slaughter civilians.

Chapter Five

15th May 2013, London, UK

"We are happy to support Libya. We stroll in to Afghanistan and Iraq. We send troops to Sierra Leone. But we totally ignore almost 100,000 deaths of innocent people in Syria! How can that be?"

A Labour MP from the north of England was standing outside the House of Commons and enjoying a chance to get a sound-bite on national television. Syria was turning into a great way to bad-mouth the Prime Minister and the Coalition on a problem where they couldn't throw back the blame to his party. It was like taking candy from a baby, as the Yanks would have it.

"So what would your party do about the situation?" the reporter asked, trying to get something new out of the interview.

"We would organise a conference between all parties and bring the conflict to an end," the MP told her. "We would not even consider putting British boots on the ground. We have lost enough young lives in recent times, so we will not make that same mistake again."

"But surely that is what both Paris and London have already proposed? Hasn't this suggestion been ignored by the various groups?"

"I'm sure you know that it's in the way it's proposed that makes the difference. If you order something then nobody wants to do it. Labour would 'invite' all parties. It's called diplomacy."

He smiled into the camera, pleased with himself and not just for the points scored for his party. Self-promotion is also good for the ego.

"Mr Speaker," the people's representative addressed the House of Commons through the microphone. "With permission, I will make a statement on the conflict in Syria, which continues to worsen."

He looked down at the prepared words in front of him. "The Syrian regime's military offensive against opposition-held areas around Damascus, Homs, Idlib, Hama and Aleppo is intensifying, with complete disregard for civilian life. The death toll…"

He re-adjusted his notes and set off into an hour that outlined the situation in that country to the House, interspersing facts with wishes, and past and present horrors with future dreams. "Online footage has shown bodies heaped in the streets, and children butchered in their homes."

The normal catcalls and boos from the opposition were absent. Everyone listened to the address intently, so shocking and awful that it was. It was now also reported that chemical weapons had been used by the Assad regime, including the use of Sarin nerve agent. Both France and the UK have had samples from within the country confirming this. And this against his own people.

"Over four million Syrians are internally displaced and a total of six-point-eight million in desperate need, including three million children. It is horrifying to imagine what life must be like for these children, witnessing violence and death on a daily basis, and enduring trauma, malnutrition, disease and shattered education."

He continued with the effect of the crisis on the region as a whole and the opportunities it was producing for the extremist factions. Even people from Britain were known to have travelled there to join the fight in the name of religion.

Both Jordan and Lebanon had expressed fears that forty percent of their populations would be formed by refugees from Syria by 2014. Bombings related to the war had already happened in Turkey; UN peace keepers had been snatched from the Golan Heights; shells had been launched across the border with Lebanon; the crisis was spreading into other parts of the region, and fears were real that the whole of the Arab world could get sucked into it.

He continued explaining the massive amounts of humanitarian aid that the UK had given, not only to Syria, but also to the countries taking the strain caused by the refugee crisis. Money had also gone to Lebanon to construct observation towers on its border to try to halt the cross-border raids that were becoming a nightly occurrence.

He moved onto solutions, and proposed a conference attended by all parties, regime and rebel alike.

The Labour MP from the North smiled to himself, already seeing himself in front of a camera again and saying, 'I told you so.'

"In our view the conference, which should be held as soon as possible, should be focused on agreeing a transitional governing body, with full executive powers and formed by mutual consent, building on the agreement reached in Geneva last year."

He had thrown down the gauntlet, the invitation to come to the table. Would it be accepted?

The speech went on, emphasising that the UK had not passed arms to any party throughout the Arab Spring, but hinting that a review of this policy may be worthwhile. To many this meant the arming of the rebel forces, or at least the less extreme of them. This type of thing had backfired on many major powers in the past, including the UK and the US. Afghanistan, Iraq, Vietnam: too many examples to ignore.

The Conservative MP was almost done.

"With every week that passes we are coming closer to the collapse of Syria and a regional catastrophe, with the lives of tens of thousands more Syrians at stake. We are determined to make every effort to end the carnage, to minimise the risks to the region, and to protect the security of the United Kingdom."

Closing, he said his thanks to the House and stood down.

Major Jack Kearney sat in the corridor outside of the Whitehall office waiting to be called in and wondering what the meeting was all about. His boss had just given him a time and a place to be, and here he was. He wasn't worried: the military was like that.

He'd been back from Beirut for four months now and was missing the place. He could almost see the beautiful women passing by on the seafront in all their finery — the place looking more like a catwalk — smell the sweet smoke of the shisha and taste the succulent seafood. He missed it.

Back with the Royal Irish Regiment and working from their Palace Barracks headquarters in Holywood, Belfast, it had been fairly easy to grab a flight across to London the night before from Belfast City Airport. The Army had booked him a room in a Travel Inn close by: he preferred this to getting a room in the Officers Mess of one of the local units. This way he could be his own man — pretend not to be a soldier — for one night at least.

Originating from the coastal town of Bangor and being based in Holywood was great and allowed him to get home to see his folks as often as he liked. Though Northern Ireland was as 'at peace' as politicians tried to portray it, it was much safer than the country Jack had grown up in, and he had relatively good freedom of movement.

But it wasn't Beirut.

The office door opened, and a young female Corporal put her head around it. "Major Kearney?"

He stood and came forward as she held the door for him. "Thanks," he said. "Do you happen to know who I'm meeting with?"

"Sorry Sir, not for me to say."

"Understood."

He was shown to a second large wooden door, which he opened himself. Behind it was a large gleaming, wooden table. Around it sat three men. He recognized only one of them, and the fact he was meeting with him was a bit of a shock.

"Major Kearney, good of you to join us at such short notice," a man in the uniform of a full Colonel said. "Take a seat. I'm Clive Bottomsley, General Staff."

"Please call me Jack, Sir, everyone else does."

"And you call me Clive. This is a very informal gathering, even if some important people are present." He gestured to the Member of Parliament that Jack had seen on television.

"Nigel Parkinston," the man said, standing and offering his hand.

The third man stood and they shook hands. "John Ryan," he told Jack, making no reference to his position.

"So," said Clive sitting in his seat. "I guess we should tell you why you're here."

"Would be nice to know. I have to admit, I had no clues from my boss."

The MP leant forward. "You may have followed my presentation to the House recently with regard to Syria. It's sort of a follow-up to that, though I am here in more of a listening role than anything else, so just ignore me and these two gents will lead."

Jack's thoughts returned to his time waiting outside before the meeting. Syria. Could he be going back to Lebanon?

Clive was speaking again. "Following Mister Parkinston's speech, the Prime Minister has instructed us to look at the options we could take to help end the crisis in Syria. The politicians will follow the diplomacy path, trying to get all parties to the table and bash out a deal." He stopped and looked directly at Jack. "Them not succeeding in making a deal is where we have to assist. Not stopping this crisis is just not acceptable. It is not only the thousands dying now, it is the possibility of things running into the surrounding countries and then into the whole of the Middle East."

Parkinston stepped in. "It could be worse than that, Jack. Syria is now a breeding ground and training ground for extremists. If this got much more out of hand, we could be looking at the start of World War Three."

Jack's mind was racing. What did they need him here for? This was serious stuff.

The quiet man — John Ryan — put him out of his misery. "You're no doubt wondering what you are doing here," he said, smiling. Jack thought he actually found it funny. "As Clive said, we have to look at the military options and, until very recently, you were one of only a few British soldiers based in that area. We need your first-hand experience."

"But I was in Lebanon, not Syria, and it was half a year ago..."

"I think that is unimportant. You were often in the border areas and mixing with the Syrians on an almost daily basis. You are current." John looked at Clive.

"You'll be attached to a four-man think-tank from tomorrow. Anything you need for a one month stay in London we will have flown over from Belfast. Just let the girl know on the way out." Clive looked to the others, then back to Jack. "Are you OK with this? Any questions?"

"A bit shocked but give me a night to think about things. Not something I expected at all. Of course I'll do my best."

"We know you will give your all Jack," said the politician. "Apart from being the man with experience on the ground, you also have a fine record as a soldier. Don't think we selected you by chance." He smiled at the Major.

"Now go on your way and enjoy the rest of the afternoon. Please report back here at nine o'clock tomorrow to meet the rest of the team. I think you'll enjoy them."

At eight-forty Jack was shown into a room, close to where the meeting had taken place the previous lunchtime. The same young, blond Corporal opened the door to Meeting Room Number Four and invited him to enter. He noticed her perfume as he passed, and suddenly realised she was a very attractive young lady. Why did he not see that earlier?

"Would you like a coffee or tea, Sir?" she asked.

"With me it's always coffee Corps," he said. "Do they use rank in here, or is it more laid back than that?"

"Most people just call me Rosie. I guess it will be strange when I go back to a normal unit, but if you're comfortable, just use my name."

"And you call me Jack," he replied. "Us Irish are quite relaxed about these things too."

He was the first one there, so prowled around the room to kill time. It was about twenty feet long and fourteen wide, with one window, with blinds, looking out to a courtyard. One wall was covered by a large white board, in front of which were a number of coloured pens. The board also doubled as a screen with a projector unit hanging from the roof so that video as well as presentations could be shown; a cable, in the centre of the long boardroom-style table, allowed a laptop to be plugged in. Four chairs were on either side of the table with an additional one at the opposite end from the screen.

On one wall was a map of the Middle East, or at least the part containing Lebanon, Syria, Israel and the countries bordering them. He could see this was new: no marks on the map, no dust or fading. It was here for this meeting.

The other wall had three pictures, all featuring Queen Elizabeth. In the first she was inspecting a guards' division in all their ceremonial finery; the second she was on the balcony at Buckingham Palace, arm raised in a wave to her people; the third was a picture of her in front of an Apache helicopter and looked as though it had come from the Army Air Corps headquarters at Middle Wallop, Hampshire.

And that was that. He glanced at his watch. Ten to nine.

The door opened again, and Rosie came in with another man wearing the rank of Captain. He had no head-dress on, so Jack had no way of knowing which unit he belonged to.

"Coffee will be here in a second Jack," she told him. "What would you like Pete?"

"The same please," the man named Pete replied. He walked over to Jack, hand outstretched. "Pete Davies, up here on detachment from Hereford."

Jack introduced himself.

"So you're here from Palace Barracks?" Pete asked. "I spent some time there in the old days, but a bit off our map nowadays. Some good memories."

"Can I ask what it is you do in Hereford?" Jack asked. "I knew a few guys from there in the past."

"I'm Regiment," Pete told him. Most Special Air Service soldiers didn't shout about their job, they just did it. Jack knew this from experience. 'Regiment' was just a way to avoid saying 'I'm in the SAS.'

Rosie arrived with the coffees, a flask in fact. "If you don't mind I made a flask, then I can leave you all to it. There's milk and sugar, and I'll make a tea as well. Anyone like biscuits?"

"We're not going to want to leave here Rosie if you keep this up," Pete responded. She blushed and left the room.

"So how much do you know about why we're here?" Jack asked.

"Just arrived this morning, so not too much at all. Something about Syria I was informed by my boss."

Jack thought about this and was just about to recount his own meeting of the previous day when the door opened again, Rosie holding it in place. The first to come in was a woman. Her dark hair and eyes and milky coffee coloured skin told Jack she was a local from the region shown on the wall map. She wore a trousers and jacket business suit and looked like she was from a Parisian catwalk.

She was followed in by a man in a sports jacket and slacks. He had a good suntan that didn't look like it had come from a beach in Spain, a darker deeper colour that looked burnt into him. Something you would get from time in the desert perhaps.

"I'll let you do your own introductions if you don't mind," Rosie told them. "If you need anything, just let me know. Jack knows which office I'm in."

She left and the four strangers looked at one another deciding where to start.

"Well as Rosie has given you my name, I'll begin," Jack told them. "Major Jack Kearney, Royal Irish Regiment based in Belfast. I've noticed around here it's all first names, so just call me Jack."

"Pete Davies from Hereford," the SAS man volunteered. He noticed the look and realised he had to add a bit more. "Yes, you guessed. I am from the 'Who Dares Wins' crowd." He took his sand-brown beret from a trouser pocket and placed it on the table.

"Colin Rutherford, from the Babylon-on-Thames here in London." He could see not everyone knew exactly what this meant. "I with SIS, the Secret Intelligence Service, commonly wrongly called MI6. We look after foreign threats and intelligence."

The others looked at each other, wondering what this mix of people were doing in one room.

"And I am Lilia Al Khatib, a widow from Syria. I got out of there about two years back when my husband was murdered at the beginning of the troubles."

An uneasy silence descended on the room. "I do not mean to shock you," Lilia carried on. "I have not worked since I came here, but my ex-husband was from your military and spent time in Syria training the same people that are now destroying our land. He loved the place and settled there. In the end, it cost him his life."

Jack stepped forward and shook her hand. "We are not judging you Lilia," he said. "I think I speak for the rest of us in saying that we seem to have a strange mix of people here. I just wonder what the thinking behind this is."

The rest also came forward and shook hands. Pete suggested they all grab a coffee. He lined up the cups and began pouring.

Just then Clive Bottomsley and John Ryan walked in.

"Good to see you are all getting along," Clive boomed. "I'm on General Staff here and basically hosting this get-together." He introduced himself and John, avoiding accurate job descriptions Jack noted. They both took a coffee and all sat down, Clive taking the head of the table.

"I guess you're all wondering why you're here, perhaps with the exception of Jack here. He spent a little time with us yesterday, and we'd like him to head the group."

John frowned and decided to talk. "He is the one with most recent experience here. He was based in Lebanon less than six months ago."

The others looked at Jack, still confused.

"The crisis in Syria has been running for over two years now," Clive started. "What is happening there is despicable, and at last our politicians have started wanting to resolve it and not just talk. Of course their role is to talk, and to try and find a diplomatic route to end things." He sipped his coffee. "But they now also agree we should have a plan in place for — shall we say — 'alternative actions' should diplomacy fail."

He gazed around the table.

"We feel you all can bring something to the party. Jack is the most current and knows how the Lebanese are reacting to the spills over the border by both the Syrian Army and the rebel forces. He knows some of their strengths and weaknesses."

He indicated Pete. "Our SAS man here has spent time in the region, but mainly in Oman and Abu Dhabi training local forces, so he knows the mentality of the people and the tactical possibilities.

"Colin comes from the Middle East desk of MI6 or the SIS as you prefer. He was based in their Riyadh agency for a number of years, and also had a spell in Bahrain during the unrest that was so glibly called the Arab Spring."

He looked then to Lilia. "And then there's Lilia here. She has suffered most from the horrors that are still occurring in her country. Her husband was one of our military instructors on a training exchange when Mister Assad was still a friend. He settled there but was considered out-spoken by the Syrian military. It cost him his life."

He took a sip of his coffee. "I'm sorry Lilia, but they must know the truth. You also worked in the Assad government, so you have an insight in to the mind of both the organisation and the people there. You also have a personal reason to make a workable back-up plan should politics fail."

John put down his cup and looked at them all, still the quiet man. Clive continued.

"We have a budget to employ you on our books for one month. In that time we would like you to put together a few possible scenarios that could be acted out if they gain Government approval. They can be anything you want, from an all-out invasion of Syria, to taking out the President. We'd also like you to consider the reactions to your suggested actions. Will the rest of the Arab world turn against us? Will we create a power vacuum as we did taking out Saddam in Iraq?"

John finally spoke. "Nothing is off the cards. If it comes to a military solution, then the best way is the way we need. Standing back watching thousands of civilians getting slaughtered is simply no longer an option." He looked to Lilia. "I'm just sorry it took so long for us to wake up."

John and Clive left the room about fifteen minutes later after explaining the resources available to the team. Laptops were brought in, documents would be made available, latest satellite imagery was possible.

"Lilia, gentlemen," Jack spoke softly to them. "I feel we have been tasked with trying to find a way to put the Middle East right again. We can all see that we bring a blend of unique experiences together here. I'm not sure why they asked me to lead, but let's just be clear from the start: everyone here is on the same level until they prove otherwise. We work together and we all have the same goal."

"I'm with you, boss," Pete said.

"Me too," said Colin.

"If it's good for my country, you will get my full support," added Lilia.

"So where do we start?"

Chapter Six

10th June 2013, Doha, Qatar

The conference was being held in an Arab state to try and provide a neutral ground to discuss the growing problems in Syria. It was thought that a place like Qatar might feel 'home' enough to get all parties to the table.

One of the senior Royal Family members, who was also high-up in the Qatari government, hosted the meeting. Again it was felt that having an Arab rather than a Westerner leading the discussions would be preferable in the region. If the drive for peace was coming from like-minded persons and with the same religious drivers, maybe it could work. And with all of its oil, the country could very well afford to foot the bill, unlike some of the European states right now.

The United Nations Secretary General attended to show the importance and levity of the meeting to the international community. Ban Ki-moon had taken over from Kofi Annan in 2006, so he was a man with a track record and a lot of respect.

All of the Gulf States sent a senior government member, along with Jordan, Lebanon and Egypt from the Red Sea and Mediterranean side of the world.

The UK, Germany, the USA, France, Holland and Spain sent representatives. This may have been an error of judgment: this was an Arab conference to settle a problem of one of their own. In private maybe they could have done more. The Arabs are a proud people, so surrendering to demands from outside was no easy thing.

Sudan opted out, saying that Syria should decide for itself how to handle internal problems, and not be bossed by the other Arab countries, who Sudan said were, anyway, only doing the bidding of the US.

Neither side of the divide in Syria attended. It made the conference less than worthless.

In the Rotana Oryx Hotel, after the day's meeting and the official conference dinner, the Westerners made their way to a jazz club on the hotel ground floor. It served beer at about six pounds sterling a pint, making even the Londoners squirm, but the music was OK and you had to find somewhere to let your hair down, didn't you?

The MP from Deptford took a long swig on his pint of German Erdinger beer. "That's better. Can't stand the official dinners over here. No booze at all. Bloody boring."

The Yank from Connecticut, standing on his left, nodded in agreement. He didn't like the Brits, but sometimes they had a point. "Dry enough out here in the desert without them stopping us drinking. Especially after a day like today. We achieved zilch."

The German spoke up. "Ja, that was a total waste of a day."

"How do you expect to make any progress if the main troublemakers boycott the meeting?" the American said. "If they can't discuss the problem, we can't solve it."

"So what do you think we achieve tomorrow?" asked the Brit.

"Nothing," said the German. "It will be another around-in-circles chat about nothing."

"Then we might as well get wasted then," from the Yank. "Otherwise we'll be bored bloody senseless in the morning."

"Hear, hear," came from the man from Deptford raising his glass. "I'll go with that."

The representative from Lebanon was on the microphone, finally reaching his point after orbiting it for a full ten minutes.

"We are already experiencing cross-border raids in to our country, mainly by the rebel forces in Syria, but also by Assad's troops. They are stealing the food and drink from the aid stations, raping our women, murdering our men. Neither we nor the UN stationed there can control such a long border with any certainty. And this is true for all of the countries surrounding the crisis, perhaps with the exception of those to the south." He referred to Israel, but to mention their name directly was akin to swearing at such a meeting.

"If the situation is allowed to spill into all of the surrounding countries, what do we have? We have a Middle Eastern War on our hands. Imagine if Turkey becomes fully involved? What do we have then ladies and gents?" He paused for dramatic effect, then continued. "We have the beginnings of World War Three."

Back at the hotel at lunchtime, the conference done, the Western delegates again came together to digest the facts from the final morning session and compare their views.

"That was a strong speech by the delegate from Beirut this morning," the Dutchman said.

"He only said what everyone else was avoiding," said the Connecticut man. "It's easy to pussyfoot around, but at the end of the day, this is about how big this damned thing can get."

"He's right though. If Turkey gets into it, then Europe is in it too."

"And I guess the States are also in it too," said the Englishman.

"How so that?" asked the Yank. "We're still far away from all of this."

"Because then it becomes bigger than a war between rival clans, a battle between different interpretations of Islam." The Englishman paused, trying to get the right words. "It becomes a kind of crusade in reverse. It's a battle of Islamic faith against the Christian faith, but with the battle moving away from the Holy Land, not moving to it."

"But we are still the other side of the bloody Atlantic!" the American pointed out, smiling. "Doesn't directly affect us at all."

The British Member of Parliament thought a second, again looking for the best presentation. "If I look at my own country," he began. "I already see tensions there between — shall we say — the Christian community and the other denominations, especially the Muslims. We have hate preachers in our streets, people recruiting for the jihad outside of our land. How will they react to a battle of Christians against Muslims moving over to Europe? Will they hide, or will they press on with their hate campaigns? And is this picture also true of your own countries?" he threw at the others.

The group of Westerners were quiet for a while. The American broke the silence.

"You got a point there bro."

The meeting reports that hit most Western capitals the next morning were more or less based on the conversation in the Rotana Oryx Hotel, rather than the content of the speeches from the delegates. They painted a gloomy picture.

Chapter Seven

15th June 2013, London, UK

"So the month is up chaps, and it's time to see what you have dreamed up," Clive said smiling. "As you can see, we have also been joined by our Government representative for the de-brief, but he is only here in a listening role to assist in his policy decisions."

"Correct," the MP told them. "Don't mind me. Speak as if I am not here and I'll try and keep quiet until the end of your presentation."

Jack stood to begin. "Please accept that we have tried to cover a number of alternatives in a fairly short space of time, so this is by no means a polished presentation. What we hope to do is give you some choices, and the pros and cons for each of them."

He flicked a remote control and a PowerPoint presentation appeared on the whiteboard.

"Option One is to send in ground troops and take control of the whole of Syria, putting a coalition government in place that would be a mix of all the major players there. This would raise any number of problems, so I'll cover them in turn. Please ask questions as we go along. A full written report will be handed out at the end anyway.

"The first problem with this course of action is the size of the Syrian Army. Pre-Arab Spring, the size of this well-armed force was estimated at half a million full-time and reservist soldiers. There have been claims of up to a thousand generals leaving and ten to twenty thousand troop defections to the rebels per month recently, but we cannot confirm these figures. We also have no idea whether they would re-unite if invaded by outsiders.

"To take on a force of, let's say, 400,000 men, we should really have an invading army strength of about one-point-two million men. After recent conflicts in Iraq and Afghanistan, we here do not think that the general public would support that type of commitment. I'm sure Mister Hague knows that better than we do.

"I have already mentioned that the force is well armed, and we have reports that they have used Scud missiles, Sarin gas and cluster bombs on their own people. This means they would probably not think twice about using them on foreigners.

"Then we must look at who would make up this one million plus force. It will certainly depend largely on persuading America to put boots on the ground, then the next main contributor would be us. France may take part, as may Holland, Germany, Denmark and others, but their contributions will be limited in numbers and probably not to the supply of fighting troops.

"We, here, do not believe that the Arab Nations will volunteer military to fight against fellow Muslims. This may be a wrong assumption, but this is our belief.

"Who could turn against us? Possibly the whole Arab Middle Eastern community in our view. Not just regionally, but within our own countries. Look at the way feelings are running high since that soldier was murdered in Woolwich. We are already seeing tit-for-tat attacks on properties, and this would become much worse.

"The Russians still maintain a naval base in the port of Tartous and have weapons supply contracts tied to this. They have vetoed everything regarding Syria since the beginning of the conflict, so we can count on them not supporting such an invasion. We also believe China would oppose any military intervention from our people.

"Foreign fighters are already reported to be operating with Assad. The Mujahideen, the Hezbollah, the Shabiha, are all said to support the Assad cause and are reportedly fighting or assisting the Syrian Army. More of their numbers would join the battle against us.

"There is more detail in the write-up but I think you get the message. Option One is out, in our opinion."

He stopped and took a gulp from a plastic water bottle.

"So Option Two. Arm the rebels. This was done in various conflicts over the years with varying degrees of success. And sometimes it comes back to bite us — take Afghanistan and Iraq for example. We made the Afghans stronger in our battle against the spread of communism, but now they are our public enemy number one through the Taliban.

"The other problem we have in Syria was touched on earlier: the Russians supply Assad. If we supply the rebels and Russia continues to supply Assad, we effectively come head-to-head with Russia."

"A little like stepping back in time," John said drily.

"Yes it is," Colin said. "Maybe good for the SIS. A new cold war."

Jack went on. "The actual arming isn't a problem. We could import the weapons through Beirut or Tripoli in Lebanon and cross the border just about anywhere. It's just the implications."

"So are we saying that Option Two is out?"

"We believe so," Jack said. "Too many negatives again."

The parliamentarian nodded his agreement. "Any other options?"

"Option Three." Pete said. "But this one is a little extreme."

"But the only one that can succeed," added Lilia, looking to Jack.

"Let's hear it," Clive said.

Twenty-five minutes later Clive and John left the room with the Member of Parliament. They had called a time out, a chance for them to talk about what the team had outlined and a chance for the team to reflect on their recommendations and have some lunch. Rosie had organised sandwiches and drinks, so the four of them were sitting around the table eating.

"How do you think it went?" asked Jack. "Do you think it's what they wanted to hear?"

"For a month studying the subject, I'd say it was a pretty comprehensive brief," Colin told him. "I sit in on a few things similar to this, and quite often the information takes months to assemble and doesn't end up recommending anything."

"It is all 'broad-brush' stuff right now," said Pete. "Whichever course they may take will need a lot of detailed planning still."

"We did fine," Lilia said. "We were asked for possible solutions, and we offered some. Now they have to decide how they go forward. I just hope they don't take too long deliberating. The country is coming apart at the seams."

"That much is true. It's a time for action and not words."

"Thanks for that Jack," said Lilia. "I think we all understand each other very well after a month together. You all give me a lot of hope for my country."

Jack looked down and took a bite of his sandwich. He liked Lilia and felt for her: it was her country that was being crucified. He wished he could help more.

"So what did you think of the presentation?" Clive asked.

The Government figure thought awhile before answering, always a man who was careful with his words. "There was little in the courses of action that we hadn't already thought about, but some of the thoughts on the possible fall-out from the various options were new to me. I feel that some of the potential results automatically disqualify both of the first two options."

Clive was nodding. "Agreed. Another war for our troops would be one too far, especially with all the defence cuts of recent years. And the public would hammer the Government for it."

"And starting some sort of an arms race with Russia to supply the two sides just means that the massacre we have now becomes forever bigger," John added. "Just imagine the destruction we would see if both sides had more modern weaponry."

"So that just leaves Option Three," Clive put in.

"Which means we need to keep the team on and begin planning the details. Do you think we have any problem keeping them on?"

"Lilia is an independent, so I cannot speak for her, but the military and SIS men will be no problem to organise. I'll have words with the relevant persons later today." This from the MP.

"So, Option Three," Clive concluded. "The assassination of President Bashar Al-Assad."

Chapter Eight

16th June 2013, outside of Aleppo, Syria

The Syrian colonel looked down at the — unsurprisingly — red button on the launch pad. Already the key switch had been made and the computer code he had obtained from officers far senior to him and close the President in Damascus had been entered into the missile control system. Distances, trajectories and co-ordinates had long since been calculated. The final step in the whole sequence was for him to simply press the button. The job of a single finger.

And then another Scud missile would begin its flight to somewhere in downtown Aleppo.

He was a loyal Assad man, a man also of the Syrian minority Shi'ite form of Islam, and of the same Alawite clan as his President, but somehow shelling civilians — even Sunni Muslims — did not seem right to him. It was not why he had joined the army.

At the same time he knew it was essential. His brothers in arms were losing badly in the built-up areas of Aleppo, the rebels employing hit-and-run guerrilla tactics and then disappearing into the civilian housing estates, some of the foreign factions coming in to assist the rebels, such as the Jabhat al-Nusra Front, being more than happy to sacrifice their own lives as suicide bombers. It was a dire situation.

Even so, he felt guilty.

His number two interrupted his thinking. "Sir, the infantry unit in town reports that the rebels are on the move. We either launch now or lose them. How do you wish to proceed?"

The colonel took a deep breath, delaying the decision a second or two longer.

"We support our fellow comrades," he said, leaning forward slightly and reaching for the red bump on the console. "Just pray it's the right decision."

The Scud missile motor fired-up, smoke surrounding the area at its base. It moved up the launcher, soon to be impacting in downtown Aleppo.

Majid Abdulla drove the red 2008 Ford Explorer through the northern outskirts of Aleppo. The car was not in great shape and had not seen any sort of service for over two years that the civil war had been running. He'd been filling it with poor grade diesel for months on end, and he knew the engine filters must be clogged with all sorts of rubbish from it. Not that he minded. No-one took too much notice of an old, knackered car.

He did not rush. That too attracted attention, and today was not a day when he wanted to be stopped by army or police patrols.

Majid was a member of Jabhat al-Nusra, a jihadist group labelled a terrorist organisation not only by the Syrian government, but also by the United States and many Western powers. Having ties to the Islamic State of Iraq, and claiming allegiance to Ayman al-Zawahiri, the leader of al-Qaeda, the group is extremely violent, with little concern for human life, either of its enemies or members. Though they had fought with the Free Syrian Army, many of the followers were foreign fighters and local Syrians viewed their staunch views on Sharia Law as disturbing. Some saw their use of mercenaries as an attempt by extremists to 'steal' their revolution.

He could have taken the 214 highway, but this was too much of a major route, so he stuck to the smaller roads, basically just steering due north. It was about 25 miles to his destination just to the south of a town called Azaz, and he estimated it would take forty-five minutes.

After about half an hour's driving, he heard the sound of a large helicopter from somewhere behind him. A minute later it came in to his forward field of vision. The Russian made Mil Mi-8 — codename 'Hip' in the NATO alliance — was at about two hundred feet and bleeding off speed and height as it prepared to land. The bulbous twin engine helicopter was one of the most common on the planet and had been used by Russia and her allies mainly as a transport aircraft, though this one was fitted with a large machine gun.

Within a minute it was out of sight.

He pressed on.

A chain link fence came into view five minutes later. He drove past a gate manned by a couple of armed sentries and saw the helicopter again in the distance as it taxied towards a hangar. Next to the gate he saw a sign proclaiming 'Minnigh Air Base – Home of 4th Flying Training Squadron'. Apart from the Mil helicopters, he could also see the MBB223 Flamingo Trainer aircraft parked on the other side of the field. A couple of scout cars drove around the perimeter track, their occupants obviously concerned about rebel attempts to seize the airfield.

It was soon behind him. He drove on until he found a dirt track on the left and turned into it. Parking behind some trees, he got out of the car, stretched and relieved himself. Walking back to the Ford he took a bottle of water and some binoculars from the passenger's side, then walked back a short way until he had a view of the base. It appeared as he had expected from photographs. A mess hall next to an accommodation block, and a couple of fuel tankers and cars parked close by. From his knowledge, it would be lunch in twenty-five minutes. Security would be minimal then.

Back at the car he opened the rear door and lifted a tarpaulin sheet. Under it was approximately one thousand pounds of cheap plastic explosive, not as nice to work with as Semtex, but more than sufficient to do the job he had in mind. He checked the detonators were still firmly in place, then traced the wires to the front of the car. They were terminated in a trigger unit that had been hidden under the front seat, the battery cover off and the batteries in the glove compartment.

Placing the trigger box on the passenger's seat he removed the batteries. They were brand new, but he tested them for life by fitting them in a small torch before removing them and placing them in to the box. This he positioned on his side of the passenger seat, within easy reach.

Majid drank more water and lay down on the grass under the trees, forcing his mind to go blank for a short while. He was almost asleep when his phone rang twice, then stopped ringing.

He glanced again at his watch. Time to go. He had to co-ordinate his move with others, and that meant being at the gate in ten minutes. The phone call was to synchronize the assault, giving everyone involved a zero point.

He started the car and drove out onto the main road again, watching the base and the main gate as he drew closer. Nothing appeared different from earlier.

Slowing as he neared the gate, he turned towards the sentries. He stopped at the barrier and one of them approached, weapon at the ready. His number two also had a weapon trained on Majid, but this was just standard operating procedure these days. Too many dead government troops meant no-one was taking anything at face value, and these men were no different.

"What are you doing here?" the soldier asked. "This is a military base."

"Is this the right way to Azaz?"

"You keep going that way," the man said, indicating the way Majid had come from. "About five miles."

"OK. I'll back out on to the road then." He started to reverse slowly, checking his watch again. It was time.

A rocket propelled grenade slammed into the gatehouse, blowing a hole in the far wall. Another smashed into a scout car that had stopped there for a drinks break, throwing it onto its side and setting it alight. The guard had turned towards the noise and then dived to the ground.

From the other side of the airport Majid could hear heavy machine gun fire, but he put this out of his head. He selected forward gears and hit the gas. The Explorer leapt forward, gaining speed before it hit the boom barrier, snapping it off its counterweight. No shots came at him and he continued to pick-up speed as he pointed the car towards the cookhouse. Over to his left he could see one of the Flamingo Trainers was on fire, black smoke billowing from a burning fuel tank. Behind him a couple of guards had found their wits and were pointing rifles in his direction, but he was already about three hundred meters away, so fairly safe.

He drove on.

As he neared the cookhouse area, he picked up the trigger box and turned a switch. It was now live.

The mess hall was now about six hundred and fifty feet away and troops were milling around everywhere, trying to find out what was going on and where the threat was. He drove towards a point next to the building and about one hundred and fifty feet from a fuel bowser, knocking a man over on the way. The body came over the bonnet and the head cracked the glass.

Coming off the road he pointed the car to the entrance door of the canteen, troops still spilling out of it. His speed was only about twenty miles an hour now, but it was fine.

At fifty feet from the door, he pressed a button on the control panel and he left the planet.

"Three of the Flamingos were destroyed, along with one Mil Mi-8, Sir," the Captain said into the radio. He could feel the anger of his superior in Damascus over the airwaves. "Also one scout car is totally written-off, and a bowser. And of course the kitchens too."

"Dead?"

He breathed in, controlling his breathing and hence his emotions. "Afraid we lost twenty-three men Sir."

"Shit!"

He waited, not willing to risk speaking more.

"Casualties?"

"It wasn't just the bomb Sir, but the fact that the fuel truck also exploded. About a hundred people are injured, some with major burns, some shrapnel, some will need amputations. Some minor stuff too."

"Did we get any rebels?"

"Three rebels dead in a firefight." The Captain didn't think this was a great return from the numbers he had lost. "Plus the bomber." It didn't help much, but it added to the rebel losses.

Not much of a bonus.

Bashar al-Assad looked over Damascus from the balcony of the Presidential Palace and wondered where things had gone wrong. His family had ruled Syria since 1971 after his father — General Hafez al-Assad — took power in what he had called a 'corrective revolution'. And they hadn't just ruled the country: they had totally controlled

Syria, owning the military and appointing people to positions of power loyal to the Alawite clan, the tribal group to which the al-Assad's belonged.

He had no interest in politics in those days and thought his brother would be the man to run the country after his father stood down. That wasn't to be. His brother had died in a car crash, and he became next in line to the 'throne'.

Bashar thought back to his days as a medical student in Damascus, then his move to London where he had attended the Western Eye Hospital to specialise in ophthalmology. And then his brother Bassel died and the England experience was swiftly halted. His country needed him.

There followed fast-track military training with rapid promotion to full colonel. Then in 1998 he was placed in charge of the Syrian occupation of Lebanon. When his father died in 2000, he had taken power, with re-election in 2007. But not really a democratic election he conceded to himself.

He saw the smoke rising in the centre of the city and wondered what atrocity the rebels had performed that evening.

The palace sat on top of Mount Mezzeh North, giving a wonderful view over the whole city. His father had built it, and its 340,000 square feet sat in grounds of over five million square feet and it was ringed by a security wall with watch towers. Maybe dad had already seen problems coming over quarter of a century before.

He heard a noise behind him, and turned to see his wife Asma, still looking half awake. He glanced down at his gold Rolex and noted it was still only six-fifteen in the morning.

"I hate this place," she told him. "I much prefer Tishreen." This was the older family palace in the Ar Rabwah district.

"I believe here is safer right now darling," he answered. "We also have the barracks here." The headquarters of the Republican Guard was also housed in the grounds of the palace, making it much harder for the rebels to decide on a surprise visit.

They had met in London, where Asma had been born to Syrian parents. She was a Sunni Moslem, and he a Shi'ite, and as the majority of the Syrian population are Sunnis, it had been a marriage made in heaven, creating a stability after major clashes between the two lines of Islam in the past. It had also looked good to the Western world that he had married an English Syrian, with hopes raised that this would have a positive effect on human rights in the country, and possibly a real chance of democracy.

"Do you think this bloody war will end soon?" she asked.

"If the foreign fighters and western governments would keep out of it, yes. I'm sure our people would take control and dispose of the extremists, then we could get on with life again."

"And make our country the beautiful place it once was," she added.

"It will come, my dear, it will come."

Chapter Nine

30th June 2013, London, UK

Nine-thirty in the morning, and the same team was assembled in the same room in Whitehall. The audience was also no different from the one that just over a month before had heard the three alternative solutions to end the bloodshed in Syria. They were waiting to hear the more detailed approach to the third option: the assassination of Bashar al-Assad.

"Morning gents," Jack started, addressing the visitors. "Again we are going to try and provide you a broad-brush plan of how we feel President Assad could be removed from his position. As before we will also provide a written report that will give more details, but basically we have options and we will take you through them and then explain our preference. This time though, instead of me talking endlessly, we will all do our own specialised part."

Colin Rutherford, who'd been hovering behind Jack's right shoulder came forward and Jack took a seat.

"Morning from me too," he began. "As you all know, I've come from the Middle East Desk of the SIS, so I have spent some time with my colleagues catching up with the situation there. I'll not bore you with what everyone already knows but will try and explain the latest humint we are getting from sources there." Human Intelligence was the most sought after information the spy community could ask for. Real feedback from real people on the ground.

"Of course, the word we get could be wrong, but if you get the same or similar from more than one source then there's a fair chance some of it is right. No smoke without fire, as they say.

"The general picture in the country is that no-one is trusting anyone else, friend or foe. On the Assad side for example, his troops do not trust the Hezbollah, though both fight together. The Free Syrian Army do not have any faith in the foreign insurgents either. Everyone is asking the question: what's in it for the other one? We have a mix of Sunnis, Shi'ites, Christians, Kurds – and that is just those really from Syria. We have plenty of reports of foreigners and are even certain that up to thirty people from the UK have left to fight.

"This means the whole country and the border areas of the neighbouring countries are highly unstable. On the positive side, it means that any team going in there from our people could also be viewed as more opportunists wanting to fight a war.

"The borders are leaking like sieves, refugees fleeing to the nearest country, rebels crossing at will to find safe haven after an engagement, people benefiting from the black market trade, jihadists coming to make a name for themselves or simply to get wasted and pick-up their seventy vestal virgins. This means crossing the border will not be too tough.

"Question then is: where to cross the border? I could run you around the surrounding countries but suffice to say that Israel is out and Iraq not a big favourite. Jordan also not too great as another one we would need to fly into. Better to come in by sea and not announce our presence. Turkey means traversing the whole length of Syria to get to the capital, and that's where we will find our target.

"That leaves us Lebanon gents." He sat down. Jack stood again.

"My turn again. Lebanon would be my favourite too. I know the country, and the people are supportive of us. They also worry about Syria using the civil war as an excuse to invade their home again, something no Lebanese person would wish for.

"We could come in by sea or air. If we used Beirut as the drop off, we would also have the shortest route to the capital Damascus. And half of that route we would be safe in Lebanon.

"I still know people there from my tour. I have spoken to them and also took a weekend in Beirut to get a feel for the situation. Don't worry, I was there as a tourist.

"Official border crossings are still manned but, with such a long border, we can slip around this. A decent car and we could be in Damascus within two to three hours of leaving Beirut, all things being equal."

Lilia had made her way over to Jack and waited for his nod.

"As Colin said, people from all over the world are making their way to my country, some because they believe in the cause, some because it is an adventure for them. This means not speaking the language is not an impossible issue, but I still recommend a local or Syrian speaker in the party. The right word in the right place may just save the mission. Being Sunni in a certain situation may get you killed; at the next confrontation it may save you. How many of you here could spot a Sunni from a Shi'ite?"

Glances were exchanged. "We get your point," said Clive. "We need a local."

"I am willing to be that local," Lilia said.

Jack looked at her, clearly surprised at this. "Lilia we are only here to put forward an option, not to volunteer for a mission," he told her.

"I am here for both."

Everyone started talking at once, the whole room shocked at the statements from Lilia.

"We will not accept your invitation," the Minister said above the din, silencing the room. He paused. "But at present we shall also not decline it. Go on."

Jack stared at him, not believing he'd willingly send a woman back in there when so much was wrong.

"OK," said Clive, trying to calm things down. "What is the plan if you should manage to get as far as Damascus?"

Jack took a deep breath, exhaled noisily.

"Should the infiltration group get to Damascus," he said, deliberately avoiding using any word that implied he or they were going in. "Then they will need a place to lie up and assess their next move. It is here that we have the least up-to-date information.

"Based on what they actually find there, they will take one of a number of courses of action. Pete, as the expert in this area, over to you."

The SAS man stepped up and began outlining different ways to take down the Syrian President.

"The way they present it, it actually sounds doable," Clive said to John and the Foreign Secretary. "OK, there are definitely risks and uncertainties, but if it came off…"

"And if the team were to be caught?" asked John. "How would the government handle that?"

The Cabinet Minister shifted uncomfortably. "We have little communication or control over Assad right now, same as all of the Western powers. I'm not sure we could promise anything."

"What about approaching the Russians? Assad still listens to them."

"I wouldn't count on that, and what if it isn't Assad troops who pick them up? As they just told us, the mix of militia in there right now is frightening."

They were all sitting in Clive's office, their coffees getting cold in front of them.

"So where do we go from here?" Clive asked.

"Hold the team together here for a couple of days and I'll have the answer. Ask them to keep fine-tuning things." The MP looked at his watch. "I'll try and fix a meeting with the PM for this afternoon. If not, first thing tomorrow."

"You've got it."

"Charles you understand we can be no part of this operation," the PM said. "Those days of taking out targets are long gone and we try and carry out espionage in a 'clean' way now."

"So you'd prefer we put boots on the ground, or just do nothing?" the Minister asked, his voice showing his frustration. "I'm not being funny, but we make all the right noises in the House, but what do we do? People have been dying for a long time out there now."

Silence.

"Do only what is necessary. You know the rules and the Government's position on intervention."

"Thanks."

The senior minister left the office seething. He knew the rules, but that didn't mean he had to like them. He only wished he had been born sooner and served under Thatcher, a PM with real balls.

He made his call.

"So what's your view to using Lilia?" Clive asked John.

"She's a local, she worked in the Assad administration and has a good reason to want to see the end of the man… A few good reasons. Do we have anyone better?"

"Not really, but she has no military training, or undercover background. It would be like dropping a lamb into a lion's cage."

"Yes, but who else do we have? She is also a woman, and the main team would be men. Would help to lower their profile a bit."

Clive thought about this. "What about the rest of them?"

Now it was John who was thinking. "You mean use the team, not just for the planning?"

"Why not? Two are soldiers, one at least with all the skill sets required, and the other with time on the ground there. Could work."

"What about Colin Rutherford?"

"We'd need someone to control and link to the UK, why not someone who has been there?"

"I feel sorry for them already," John said.

"But you saw their reaction when Lilia volunteered. They feel responsible for one another after only two months together."

"God help them."

Clive and John had just left the meeting room and the team sat momentarily in silence, looking at their writing pads or the empty desk areas in front of them. What they had just heard was not something that they'd expected.

Lilia broke the silence. "You all know that I will do it, but it's my country. I don't expect you to do the same."

Pete looked at her. "I am a professional soldier Lilia, and I understand more than most what they are asking of us. It will not be easy, and if Assad's people, the rebels or any of the million and one other idiots roaming your country right now catch us, it won't be pretty." He looked about the rest of the group, eyes hard. "I know people in our lot who have been caught and interrogated in places like Iraq. What you see on telly is only half the story."

Colin spoke. "Pete is right Lilia. This isn't a game. We get reports of some of the stuff that's going on, and it is nothing less than barbarous."

"As I said, it is my country, my home. I cannot sit on the fence any longer," Lilia said, standing.

"Sit down! Wait!" It was Jack, himself now on his feet. "I know every observation you've all made is right, but we need to think about this carefully. If we do not accept this, then someone else has to go along with it, and they have to try and make our plan work. If it does, great. If it doesn't, then I personally will feel responsible for those poor bastards."

He sat down and everyone looked to him. "I am not happy to go, but I believe that I have as much chance as anyone one else. I'm with Lilia."

A smile spread across the face of the Syrian woman. "Thank you Jack."

Pete smacked his fist on the desk. "You are both bloody idiots. I'm coming too."

All eyes turned on Colin. "I guess I must be the guy we proposed is the link man based in Lebanon," he said. "That's if you'll have me?"

They were all on their feet now, coming together like players before an important rugby game.

After a minute, Jack broke away. "I suppose I'd better let John and Clive know the bad news then."

Chapter Ten

5th August 2013, Hereford, UK

The sound of the nine-millimetre pistol discharging another round echoed around the indoor range, and the target fifty feet away grew a new hole in the body area. Lilia lowered the weapon, taking off the empty magazine and checking the internals were clear. Pete looked over her shoulder.

"Clear," he announced.

John and Jack came forward and together the four of them walked up the range to the target.

"Wouldn't fancy meeting you in a dark alley in a bad mood," Pete said, looking at the grouping. "This one is dead."

"It's the first time a man has said that to me," Lilia quipped. "Normally you guys are trying to get me in to the alley in the first place."

They all grinned. A month of training in the SAS barracks had allowed the soldiers amongst them to hone their skills, and the others to learn some new ones. Lilia and Colin had focused on fitness and the pistol — it was years since Colin had fired one, nowadays he was a desk-driver — while the main focus for Pete and Jack had been brushing up on their basic Arabic. All had done a crash course in first aid, and condensed sessions on 'escape and evasion' and 'handling interrogation'. The rest of the time was spent fine-tuning the plan and playing 'what if?' games. They hoped they had now covered all eventualities, but all were realistic enough to know this was not possible.

They were a tight team now.

"Let's call it a day," Jack told them. "I could murder a beer."

They cadged a lift into town after showering and changing. It was a beautiful September evening, one of the few the UK had seen this year so far. They were dropped in the town and headed for a pub called from the Weatherspoon group, called the Kings Fee. It had a nice outdoor seating area and the beer was cheap.

"Clive and John are coming down tomorrow," Jack told them. "Just got a call from them before we left. Won't discuss anything on the phone, but I can guess it means things are moving."

"Or the powers that be have called it off," said Colin. "That's not unusual. Planning, training, then someone in some office somewhere decides it's not such a great idea."

The men supped their beer, Lilia preferring white wine.

"Do you think that's why they are coming Colin?" Lilia asked. "You don't think they could have informed us it was all off over the phone?"

Colin thought a moment. "You could be right. Easier, if it is off, to call us up to London and send us on our way after signing a few non-disclosure forms. You could be right."

"Woman's intuition," she smiled.

Pete went up to the bar for another round, stopping to speak to another member of the elite regiment. It was strange how they all just looked like normal civilians, Jack thought. Especially Pete, who hadn't shaved or had a haircut for the last four weeks in preparation for the trip to Syria. Colin and himself looked similar.

Colin's phone rang and he excused himself to speak to his wife in London. He was the only one of them with a partner. Jack was pleased that he would be based outside of the 'danger zone.'

"What are you thinking?" Lilia asked.

"Not too much really. Just that Colin will at least be outside of Syria, and he is the married man. The rest of us are single, so less problem if things go awry." He reddened and started again. "Sorry Lilia. Of course you were married and I should have thought before I spoke."

"It was a long time ago now Jack. Don't be sorry. I have fond memories of my husband, but I am also ready to move on with my life." She smiled at him. "If I ever find the right man."

"I'm sure you will one day. You're very pretty."

"Maybe I already have." She gave him a mysterious smile and excused herself to the ladies.

Left to himself, Jack had a chance to reflect on the remark and the look. He somehow felt that it was personal and pointed at him but had no idea why he felt this way.

Jack picked up and sipped his third coffee of the day as they waited for Clive and John to make their appearance. They should have been in the barracks at nine o'clock, but an accident on the M4 motorway had delayed them. It was hoped that nine-thirty would see their entrance.

Pete was nursing a bit of a headache, having stayed on with one or two of his pals when the others had left at ten o'clock. He had his feet on a chair and was half asleep.

Lilia was surfing the net, reading the latest atrocities that were occurring in her home country.

Colin just paced by the window. He seemed anxious to be home since the call the previous evening. Maybe the kids were playing up?

Jack drank a little more coffee. He heard a car. "Is that them, Colin?"

Colin looked out the window. "One second, can't see inside the car. Yes, that's Clive out. And John."

"Good. Soon get on with things."

Pete sucked on a bottle of water and rubbed his eyes. The hangover wasn't so bad anymore. "Why didn't you guys take me home with you?" he complained.

"If you can't handle it, you shouldn't try it," Lilia told him.

"That's what mum used to say," Pete told her. "But dad always said, 'if it doesn't kill you, it makes you stronger.' Wish I'd taken more notice of mum last night."

They all laughed, just as Clive and John walked in.

"We're not that funny," John said, smiling for probably the first time they'd seen. "And when we finish here you might stop laughing for a while."

"That bad?" asked Jack.

"Depends how you look at it," Clive joined in. "We want you to fly in to Beirut and start execution in two days."

"Perfect," Pete told them. "Probably no alcohol there."

"You might be disappointed there," Jack said. "I know a few wee haunts we can try…"

Again a round of laughter and they sat down. "Let's try and get through this quickly," Clive said. "Then you can all get away to your homes and families for forty-eight hours before we get on with the show. John and I will be joining you as far as Lebanon."

"You've got them worried Pete. They think you might get drunk on the plane!"

"I might at that."

After the meeting, Clive and John jumped in the car back to London, Colin grabbing a lift from them as he'd left his car with his wife. Pete also caught a lift with them to the local station, where he bought a ticket to Manchester to see the family.

"So what are your plans Jack?" Lilia asked. "No family to see?"

"Mum and dad in Bangor, next to Belfast, but for two days not really worth it. I'll probably grab the train to London and have a nice meal."

"That sounds like a plan. Mind if I join you?"

Jack hesitated before answering, thinking back to the night before. "Sure, if you like. I have no hotel booked or anything else, so it's going to be a little bit haphazard."

"Right now Jack, I've got this team and nothing else, so if you'll let me tag along, I'd love it."

At those words, he felt incredibly sorry for her. She had lost so much, yet she was so good. "You're more than welcome. Not saying I'm great company or anything, but let's call it a 'team bonding' exercise."

"I'll just pack my things," Lilia said. "Then meet you at the gate in fifteen minutes."

It was three fifteen that afternoon that they got off the train in Paddington Station and took a taxi to the nearby Landmark Hotel on Marylebone Road. It wasn't the cheapest hotel in the world, but they both decided that it could be a while before they stayed somewhere so extravagant again. And, anyway, the MOD had said they would pick-up the tab for the leave.

After checking into their rooms and freshening up, they met in the centrally located Gazebo Bar.

"Wine?" Jack asked.

"But of course," Lilia agreed. "Will we stay here for dinner, or do you fancy something different? A good Lebanese meal to prepare for the trip?"

"Why not. Do you know somewhere good?"

"I know a place in Baker Street if you're interested."

They both had a glass of white wine, then caught a cab the short journey to Baker Street. Lilia ordered, though Jack obviously knew his food well from his time in Beirut. With the meal they took a bottle of the Lebanese white from the Beqaa Valley.

"Not many people realize that Lebanon was one of the first wine producers," Lilia told him. "And it tastes as good as the French stuff."

Finishing the meal with sticky Lebanese sweets, both were full and slightly tipsy.

"A nightcap somewhere, or are you done?" Jack asked.

"I think one more won't kill me."

"I'm sure Pete thought the same last night," Jack warned. "But OK, let's take a chance."

They found a bar around the corner and Jack ordered another wine for Lilia and a beer for himself. He was starting to feel slightly wobbly, but the company meant that he didn't care too much about it. Turning, he found Lilia had found a quiet corner for the two of them and he carried the drinks across, dodging people, far more wobbly than he was, along the way.

"To our little adventure." Lilia toasted. "That it comes off and we are able to repeat this afterwards."

Jack returned the toast but wondered if it was a little heavy. He sipped the beer. "Will you return to Syria when things get back to normal?" he asked.

"If things get back to normal, you mean."

"They will one day."

She pondered this one. "I don't know Jack," she said. "I quite like England now. I guess it depends where I see my life. And that depends on who I have in it." Again the mischievous and secretive grin. "Do you know anyone?"

Again Jack felt the finger pointing his way. He didn't have too many liaisons with ladies, so he was a little nervous.

"Just kidding around Jack. Keep calm!" She grabbed his elbow and pulled him closer. "But you are good company."

"And you are too."

She looked up in to his face. "I like you Jack. We've worked together for three months now and I think I know you. You are the first man I have felt close to for a long time."

"I like you too Lilia, but I don't know if this is a good time for a relationship."

"When is a good time?" she asked. She pulled his head to her and kissed him. He returned the kiss, half wondering if this would have happened if he hadn't been drinking. But right now, he knew he didn't actually care.

Chapter Eleven

16th August 2013, Damascus, Syria

Ahmed led his force of seven rebel soldiers through the rubble, avoiding main roads. It was dark, so they did not need to worry about the Syrian Air Force jets and helicopters that swooped on them with rockets and bombs during daytime. They had no air support, so this made any daylight raids terribly one-sided, meaning that most of the action was under the cover of darkness.

He had just turned fifteen now, and in the present circumstances considered himself very much a man. It had been nine months since he had turned to the gun, and he already had many government troops to his name.

He wore a pair of camouflage trousers over a pair of Adidas training shoes, a black T-shirt and sleeveless jacket with large pockets filled with boxed rounds and magazines. A couple of grenades he'd taken from a dead Syrian Army soldier were in his top pocket, and an AK47 hung on his right shoulder. A few wisps of facial hair sprouted from his chin.

Ahead of him he noted that the rubble was ending, so he motioned everyone to stop while he scouted ahead looking for problems or another way to avoid the clearing.

Crawling up behind the last pieces of cover, he slowly scanned the area from left to right and then back the other way. Nothing, but something didn't seem right. Too quiet, if that was possible, or maybe just a kind of sixth sense that he had learned to trust.

To his left, maybe a hundred feet away, was more rubble and broken buildings. They gave cover the way his party wanted to go. By back-tracking a little, he could move in to the line of what was once houses without exposing his people in the clearing. He decided this was the best course of action and signalled for his men to back-up.

Something inside of him was still bothering him though. He decided not to ignore it.

He called his men in to a small circle, all dropping to their haunches and listening carefully.

"I think there is an ambush ahead," he whispered. "I can see nothing, but I can feel something."

One of the others nodded. "Me too. Too quiet."

"Something like that," he agreed. "So we split in two and one goes either side of the clearance, carefully through the rubble. It may be nothing, but better safe than sorry."

He sent four men right and he and two others followed the line of rubble on the left.

After moving slowly forward for about eighty paces he stopped and climbed the pile of concrete and bricks. As he reached close to the top he edged upwards even more slowly, eventually turning his head and raising just one eye above the debris.

He was just beyond the clear area. To his right behind a pile of rubble was an armoured car with a heavy machine gun mounted on top. If they had entered the clearing they would have been mown down. All seven of them. But now the tables were turned and they were the hunters.

He had no radios to communicate with the other half of the patrol, so he sent a man to fetch them. After ten minutes all seven of them were squatted down in the dirt about a hundred feet and a large half-collapsed building away from the enemy position.

"There is only the one vehicle," he told them. "Maybe a second one is close by, but not close enough to bother us."

"What do you intend Ahmed?"

"We'll blow it up of course."

"With what? We have no RPGs."

"I have two grenades," he told them. "And if we're lucky, this will only need one. But we must have a route out if we do this, as it will certainly attract others if they are in the area."

"I know a cellar not five minutes from here," one of the men volunteered. "It used to be a friend's house."

"OK. This is what we do." Ahmed outlined his plan.

Briefing over, the four-man group climbed up the rubble heap where Ahmed had first spied the vehicle, taking position just below the summit to allow them to give covering fire if needed. The other three moved to another piece of cover close to the rear of the armoured car.

"You two must cover me," Ahmed told them, noting that one of the guys was only about thirteen years of age. "I will do the deed."

With the two positioned, he moved from shadow to shadow until he was close to the car. Now there were no more places to hide. He took out one of the grenades, checking that the pin and the trigger arm were in place. He placed his AK47 on the ground to give him a free hand. Then he studied the vehicle again.

Though he didn't know the make, he knew it was Russian. Some of the older fighters he had met were Syrian military deserters, and they had taught him about some of the hardware Assad's men were using. He knew about the dangers of the tanks, helicopters, cars and the rest. He also had learned from them about the weaknesses.

The biggest weakness of the vehicle in front of him now, was that it had no real rear view to speak of. And he was behind it.

He moved forward stealthily, stepping from toe to toe. He reached the rear of the fighting vehicle. He had two choices: blow a wheel off and cripple it; drop the grenade inside and kill it. The second was a more risky option and meant climbing onto the hulk. This could alert those inside and then his war would be over.

He decided on the second option.

He looked at the rear wall of the car. A spare wheel was mounted on it, about three feet up. If he used this to climb up, he could step off it onto the flat area behind the turret.

Ahmed was young, carrying not a picking of fat, and easily hauled his body up the tyre, the rubber damping any sound from the movement. He shoved a foot into the wheel hub area and pushed his head over the top of the rear gratings, the sound of the idling engine close to his ears, drowning out all other noise. He could see a hatch cover on top of the turret, but it was closed. Where could he put the grenade in? Was the hatch locked from the inside? Was there a viewing slit he could use?

The revs of the engine suddenly increased, and he heard something happening inside, perhaps a gear being selected to move off. He had to move now.

He stepped on to the back of the vehicle and moved forward, all stealth gone. He hoped that the engine noise would cover him, but time was, in any case, against him, so it was now or never. In three steps he was at the turret. He leaned forward to try the hatch, but it was tagged from the inside. Shit!

It was then he saw the viewing slit for the commander. He ripped out the pin from the grenade, released the trigger arm and pushed it through the gap in the armour. He heard a yell from inside, but he was already leaping off the superstructure and onto the ground, running again to the rear of the vehicle, putting distance between him and the explosion.

Whummpf! The grenade had worked and he could imagine the carnage in the small space inside the armoured car. Smoke poured from slits and holes in the structure and the engine revs returned to idle. The vehicle was dead. So were its occupants.

It was three o'clock in the morning and he woke himself up with his screams. It didn't happen every night, but it did happen often. Sometimes it was a dream from over a year before when his mother and his darling Saumaya had been raped to death. Sometimes he had been captured by Assad's men and was having his finger nails hauled out of their beds, the pain unimaginable, even in the nightmare.

Tonight it was the men in the armoured car burning to death, but it was he who was experiencing the intense heat and no way to escape it, locked inside the steel coffin.

He got up off the mattress formed of sacks on the basement floor. Above him, the house that used to own the cellar was a pile of rubble. To get in you had to climb the heap of bricks and find a hole that led to the top of the stairs. It was hard to find if you didn't know where to look.

At fifteen years of age, Ahmed had seen far too many bad things in his life. He wondered each day if it would be his last, and he would join Saumaya in another place called Paradise, but part of him admitted that this couldn't really exist. What sort of a God would allow all of these horrible things to happen? Surely nothing so sacred would let these things go on.

He went to stairs and climbed out, descending the rubble to relieve himself. He had a drink of warm water.

Back in his bed, he tried to sleep and hoped the dreams would stay away until dawn.

Chapter Twelve

17th August 2013, Beirut, Lebanon

They stood at the base of the bronze statue to Rafik Hariri in Ain A-Mreisseh, just across the road from the St George Hotel and the marina, and almost at the spot where the man had died more than eight years before. His family had paid for the statue, the city providing the ground.

"He was a bit of a controversial figure in his time," Jack told them. "He headed five cabinets during his two stints as Prime Minister and basically got Lebanon back on its feet, but he is also implicated in much of the corruption that was going on back then. They say he was worth about fifteen billion dollars when he died."

Colin, Pete, Lilia and Jack had walked across the road from where they were staying in the Phoenicia Hotel, a chance to get away from Clive and John for a break. They'd been in Beirut two days now and needed some time out.

"Who killed him?" asked Pete.

"Depends who you believe," Jack answered. "Some would have you believe Israel, with rumours of missiles, drones and air strikes. No-one really claimed it."

"Most people — including me — believe it was because of his opposition to the Syrian Army occupying Lebanon. Assad never likes competition," Lilia informed them. "But as Jack said, nobody ever claimed responsibility, even to this day."

"Seems like the man in Damascus has always been a bit of a character," Colin said. "He always tries to be larger than life."

"His father was worse," Lilia told them. "He at least has some Western values, whether it is what he picked up from his time in London, or his dress code, or the doctor in him, he is softer than old Assad. And of course his wife is a great shopper, even today while their own people are slaughtering one another."

"I guess we should head back and get on with things. Clive seems anxious to get the operation under way."

Jack started back across the road, dodging the traffic. Lilia ran forward to him from the others and slipped a hand onto his elbow. They had decided not to tell the others of the nights in London, but anyone could see they were close.

"Are you ready Jack?" she asked.

"I'm ready. We all have to be Lilia."

"It's not too late to cancel," she said. "This is not going to be fun, and I am willing to walk away from it if you are."

Jack looked at her. "I'm pleased we met Lilia and I want things to carry on between us, but at the same time I know what we are hoping to achieve must be done. The people of your country deserve that, and you would never live with yourself if you didn't at least try."

She hugged his arm, her head resting briefly on his shoulder. "You are right. But if we get out of this in one piece, then I want to make a life with you. I feel alive again."

"That is a promise Lilia. We will stay together."

"Tomorrow we move up to the border and set you up with clothes, transport, weapons. We cannot do this here as it would give you away from the beginning. Colin, you can stay here if you wish," Clive finished.

"No Clive, I'll join the party. It helps if I see what tools they have, and what they don't have."

"Good enough. Pack for two nights away. On the second night, you guys will cross the border into Syria."

"Enjoy this evening," John told them. "It could be your last time in civilisation for a while."

He looked around the three people crossing the border, searching for any outward sign that they didn't want to go. They did not look away. "Jack, can I have a brief word once we break up?"

"Sure. I suggest folks that we all go for some food together this evening. Something close and not too late, though most places don't serve until about nine o'clock. You all up for that?"

All five in the room agreed and a time was set to meet in the bar at eight.

"OK, see you all later," Jack dismissed them, staying behind with John and Clive. The three of them sat at a small table.

"You and Lilia seem close," John said. "Be careful. It could affect your judgement."

"John, we've been together for a few months now, so yes we are getting close. It won't affect my carrying out my job. Hopefully the bad guys in Syria will also think we're close. We are pretending to be married if you recall."

John looked to Clive, who gave an almost imperceptible shake of the head: leave it.

"OK, then do you need any more from us?" Clive asked. "You will get everything on the shopping list. That you'll see tomorrow."

Jack thought a short while, going through a checklist in his head.

"I think we are as prepared as we can be," he informed them. "We will need things as we go along, but we will have to find them as we need them."

"Colin will link with us in London, so if you need more, then we will try and arrange it. It will mean you crossing the border to get it though. Maybe not a great idea."

"I guess we need to cross that bridge when we get to it. See you at eight."

The dinner was just coming to an end, the hour quickly approaching midnight. They'd all shared a seafood starter and then pigged-out on steaks, knowing it might be the last good piece of meat they would get for some time, at least for the three people crossing the border. Clive and Colin had desserts, the rest happy to just take a good cognac and coffee.

"How's the coffee in Syria Lilia?" Jack enquired. "I can't start a day without a cup."

"Normally good, but right now could be a problem," she told him. "You might have to start drinking homemade wine for breakfast."

"Things could be worse."

Clive paid the bill and they left for the hotel. "One for the road?" he asked when they got out of the taxi. "We don't leave until ten in the morning, so not too bad."

Colin excused himself, explaining he had to call home, and Lilia said it was time to turn in, but managed a secret signal to Jack first. The rest went to the bar and ordered a beer.

"Who's round is it?" asked Pete.

"I'll get them," said Jack.

"No need," said Clive. "I'll settle all the bills in the morning. Put it to the room."

"Please thank the Prime Minister when you get back to London," Pete joked, grinning broadly.

"You've got it."

An hour later they all left for the lifts to their rooms, happy but not drunk.

Jack went to his room and opened the door. Lilia lay in his bed, half asleep. "I thought you were staying out all night," she mumbled.

"No chance of that knowing you were waiting," he said. "Just didn't want to leave too early and get the others suspicious. Better you only left with Colin."

"So now they think I am having an affair with a married man?"

"John and Clive suspect something is happening between us, but to tell the truth, I don't care."

"Come here. I need you."

He came to the bed and Lilia stood, naked. She began to remove his clothing, kissing him as she did so. Soon they were both naked and forgetting all about what tomorrow was to bring.

They were on the road just after ten, in a minibus that John was driving. It was obvious from the way he drove that he had been this direction before, making Jack wonder again what his real role was in all of this. John had still not volunteered this information to any of them. Jack suspected he was something to do with Colin's lot — the SIS or MI6 — but Colin had found no-one in Babylon-on-Thames that knew of him, or at least who admitted it. There again, Colin tended to be on the desk side of the organisation, and he suspected that John was more into hands-on operations.

Winding up the hills away from Beirut they could soon look back down on the city, the Med sparkling behind it. It looked like a holiday resort, not a city on the doorstep of a war zone.

After a short while the beautiful view also disappeared.

"The roads are really good," Pete said. "I didn't expect that."

"Not too sure how good they'll be on the other side of the border though," Clive told him. "They were good, but with tanks chewing them up with their tracks and roadside bombings, things will be deteriorating. Also there has been no maintenance on them for the last years."

"True. Bloody mountainous too."

"That's why we picked you Pete. We know it's your specialty with the Regiment, that you are part of the Mountain Troop."

"I spent a little time in Afghanistan last year," Pete told them. "Compared to the locals there, us SAS boys are like snails. They're all mountain goats over there."

"Could be you're just getting old Pete," Jack joked.

"Look who's talking," said Lilia. "Old soldiers never die, they only fade away."

The minibus filled with laughter, the mood light. It was the first time they had really laughed since leaving the hotel: this was no longer just a story – they were now heading for the border and all of the troubles that were waiting there.

A sign post pointed off the main road to the border towards the town of Anjar. "That's where we are headed now and will stay tonight," John told them. "We have a battered looking four-by-four there for you, and the rest of the shopping list. Should be there in around twenty minutes."

"Where do we stay?"

"I sorted out a villa through the embassy here. They have contacts."

"So we're off the map from now on?" Jack asked.

"Basically, yes. Tomorrow night you cross in to Syria."

The moment of laughter was gone, and a stony silence fell on the van. Everyone had their own demons to contend with.

Chapter Thirteen

19th August 2013, Syrian border

Abdulla Sadik watched the border from his tower, wondering why they bothered. Everyone knew that the rebels were crossing the invisible line in the ground each night, attacking targets in Syria and then returning to the relative safety of Lebanon at the end of their mission. It was also well known that the Syrian Army were occasionally pursuing them outside of Syria when they had good intelligence of their whereabouts and wiping them out.

The gaps between the towers meant this was all easily possible without the Lebanese Army having any knowledge of it.

To the north he could see the lights of Anjar. They were far enough away to not ruin the kaleidoscope of stars that glowed above his head, but close enough to remind him that civilisation still existed.

"How long before we finish our shift?" Fatih asked him. "I'm freezing."

"Ten minutes," he replied. "Go and wake the next two."

His colleague climbed down and walked to the accommodation hut where the troops took turns sleeping. Soon he would get a few hours rest and then, with dawn, he would return to his home and family.

A couple of miles along the border, Jack, Pete and Lilia drove their ten year old 4 x 4 Range Rover, that had seen better days, along a dirt track. The vehicle had been white once, but now was flecked with rusty red and had more dents on its bodywork than it had flat panels. Under the bonnet however was a nearly new engine and transmission and according to John the thing would drive them to the UK if necessary. They all hoped it wouldn't be.

John again had puzzled them, leading the way to the dirt road but not to the border itself. For a backstage man, he certainly seemed to have plenty of field experience.

The party was alone now and driving without headlights, never getting over about ten miles an hour.

In the rear of the car, beneath a false floor in a space about nine feet square and eight inches deep, a box of grenades was stored. It also contained additional ammunition for the weapons in the main cabin area, two AK47s in keeping with the normal rebel weaponry, and three 9mm pistols, one apiece.

On the back seat next to Lilia was a film camera — nothing flash, just something that a low level crew might have for a backstreet movie company. They had decided that making a documentary about life in Damascus would be a good cover story and allow them to remain British. Lilia would be the narrator and anchor, Jack the manager and Pete the cameraman. Microphones, booms and other filming equipment were on the floor in front of the bench seat.

Their clothing and personal items were stored in the rear of the car, providing further cover for the hidden compartment. Essential gear was kept in small civilian style Bergens, just enough to give them some warm clothing and food if they had to run, but the rest was in large bright coloured cotton sacks, tied at the top. Flashy baggage would only attract attention and probably end up stolen at a check-point, therefore they travelled like normal working people from the area.

Both Jack and Pete were lucky enough to have dark hair, Jack's almost black. Having missed out on shaving for weeks now, both had longish, slightly unruly hair and trimmed beards. Not at all military-looking. They wore cargo pants, Jack's a khaki colour and Pete's a sandy shade. These were topped with faded and worn T-shirts.

Lilia's olive skin made her look like the local that she was, though her clothes and make-up were toned down from her usual glamorous looks. She wore jeans and a light round-necked pullover, disguising her slim, womanly features.

The road was slowly winding downwards, the track full of holes and ruts making driving difficult, but Pete was managing it well. It wasn't the first time he'd done this sort of thing, and the terrain reminded him of parts of Oman. Dawn was starting to break through the darkness, and in the thin grey light they could see the hardy Anti-Lebanon Mountains disappearing to their left, all the way up to Homs. On the right and in the distance stood the tallest of them all, Mount Hermon, at just over nine thousand feet. If they weren't so nervous, it would have been quite a sight to behold, but right now it was just a barren and rocky landscape, somehow threatening their very existence.

As the light came up, the rocky surrounding changed from blacks and greys to a reddish brown. Little grew up here, but in the valleys below some arable land could be made out.

After about an hour, they hit a minor but at least once tarmacked road and turned right along it. They were in Syria now and eventually could see the border post of Jdaidit Yabws. If the maps and GPS were right, they would drop onto the main Damascus-Beirut highway about half a mile past this on the Syrian side, but no-one was certain how fluid the border was or if it was normally manned since the troubles had begun.

Pete pulled over about half a mile from the border post. They all got out and stretched, slurped some fluids, then the two military men took out binoculars and scanned the land ahead.

"Looks like we come out a little closer to the border post than the maps are showing," Pete said, still studying the buildings through the field glasses.

"I didn't see any movement though," Jack said, placing his binoculars on the car bonnet. "Did you see anything?"

"I saw a cigarette end glowing, but it was on the Lebanon side, so maybe a guard walking around and having a cigarette. Couldn't really make out the person, so not too sure."

"I saw another dirt track off to the left. Maybe we should take that and pop out a bit further up?"

"You're right. We can always do a bit of cross-country in this beast if needed, but best to do it before the locals get active."

"That'll be soon," said Lilia. "They'll be up soon as the sun gets full, so best we move."

They climbed aboard the Rover and moved on, turning into the dirt track and passing a couple of ramshackle houses. Dogs barked, but no-one came out.

Twenty minutes later, after a short off-road excursion, they were on the main highway and pointing towards the city of Damascus.

The outskirts of Damascus didn't look so bad. As they passed through Yafour, people moved around the streets in the early sunlight, going to their work and shopping. Trying to continue life as normal in a country where normal had fled a few years before.

Two storey houses lined the edges of the city, the odd one at first, but building up in to an endless built-up area, just the same as it did in cities all over the world. Most were a pale yellow, looking as if they were made from sandstone. This was possibly a throwback to the way housing was built in the olden times, still able to be seen in ancient forts around Syria. It also helped to reflect the heat of the sun as the summer came on.

The Beirut-Damascus Highway turned into the Southern Bypass and the GPS informed them that their junction was approaching, so they turned off at Souk El Madin and Basatin Al Qanawat area and moved north towards the city centre.

As they got deeper in, the scenery changed and the feeling of normality went with it.

"They've really hammered this place," Pete observed. "It's a bloody mess."

"It's a shame you didn't get to see it before all of the troubles," Lilia told him. "Damascus was such a wonderful place. Cafes, restaurants, history… late nights sitting in sidewalk coffee shops putting the world to rights. Even Assad couldn't stop the people enjoying themselves."

They looked out at the passing ruins in silence.

Strange though it was in the middle of a war zone, Lilia had managed to speak to some relatives and friends who still had contacts in the capital whilst the team had trained in

73

Hereford. To everyone's surprise — including her own — it was discovered that business attempted to go on as usual. The souk was still running, shops still functioned in a limited fashion, and hotels were still taking guests.

They headed steadily north towards the Four Seasons Hotel, off Brazil Avenue.

The roads were not deserted, but Lilia assured them they were very quiet compared with before the crisis had happened. "It would have still been rush hour now," she informed them. "Would be back-to-back traffic here, every lane stopped."

"Every cloud has a silver lining," Pete said, smiling.

"Back then the only lining was the Assad family lining their pockets from what I read," Jack put in. "They had fingers in all sorts of pies, and not just the President."

"It was rumoured he was worth over five hundred million dollars before the conflict began," Lilia said. "Meanwhile people were living in the sticks on nothing."

"An old, old story, not just here in…"

"Military check point. A hundred and fifty feet ahead." They were passing an area called Al Qanawat when Pete suddenly broke into the conversation.

Jack and Lilia looked through the windscreen of the Rover and saw the soldiers on the road. Off to one side was an armoured car which the two soldiers identified as a BTR-60, a Russian built eight-wheeled armoured personnel carrier (APC) with a KPVT heavy machine-gun mounted in a small bubble style turret on the top. These APCs had been in service since the 1950s, and the Syrian Army had over six hundred of them. A soldier could be seen standing in the turret, and a further five soldiers were on the street, two to each side, stopping cars and checking passes and one overseeing the group.

The Rover crawled closer to the checkpoint, the occupants getting ever more nervous. All carried UK passports, but not in their own names. Their cover story was about to be tested, as were their passports and faked stamps for the border crossing. They had considered just doing the crossing for real, but this would have meant crossing with no weapons, or risking a search that could have exposed them.

They were only four cars back from the soldiers now. "Get the paperwork ready Lilia."

She dug in to a handbag, extracting the passports, a couple of reference letters, and a copy of their hotel booking and flight tickets home from Beirut in two weeks.

Shouting suddenly started up ahead at the checkpoint and they all strained to see what was going on.

An old red Escort was stopped next to the two troops on their side of the street. An old man was getting out of the driver's door, arms in the air. The sergeant overseeing things had a Kalashnikov trained on his stomach.

"What did he do?" Lilia asked.

"Upset them," Pete said simply.

One of the soldiers pushed into the door of the Escort, digging for something out of their sight, but down low, causing him to bend almost double. After about fifteen seconds in this position, he backed out, a nondescript pistol in his hand. He waved it above his head, triumphant.

The sergeant still had his weapon trained on the old man, but the second soldier from that side of the road was behind him. He gripped his AK47 by the barrel, and a swung it in a roundhouse arc, connecting with the back of the old-timer's head. The man went down like a sack of potatoes, blood pouring from a gash in his greying hair.

"Bastards!" growled Lilia.

The two soldiers who'd manned the checkpoint on their side of the road slung their guns over their shoulders and hooked the man under his armpits. The sergeant could be seen barking orders at them, and they moved with the unconscious body to the APC. The sergeant followed, watching them struggle with the dead weight, trying to lever the man in through the back doors of the vehicle.

"They obviously found what they were looking for," said Pete.

"Probably told to just get some subversives," said Jack." Keep the local rebels on their toes."

"To rule by fear, you must keep the people scared," Lilia told them. "I'm sure you learn that in your SAS training Pete."

"We learn many things, not all of them nice."

"I guess we will learn many more things here, and even more of them not nice," Jack added.

Ahead of them, the checkpoint was hastily packed away and the BTR-60 manoeuvred itself onto the road. It turned away from them and towards the headquarters of the Damascus Province Police on Khaled bin al-Walid Street, attacked at the outset of the uprising by the Free Syrian Army rebels, but now back in service. The Assad people were determined it would show its dominance of the locality.

"The poor bastard. God knows what's coming to him."

"Better him than us Jack," Lilia said.

They drove onwards, the checkpoint gone.

Ahmed was where he often went during the days. Nights were dangerous, not only for the fighters, but during daylight hours it was fairly safe to roam, to visit the shops with their limited provisions, to go to the parks, and to the temples from the past, to remember.

He was back at his home, now only a pile of broken masonry, but still his street, his spot, his starting point in life. Angled piles of bricks, whole walls still upright, whole walls lying at crazy angles, powdery yellow dust everywhere.

He could still see the area which had been the living room, the kitchen, where he had had breakfast before going to school. He could imagine his mother calling him, begging him to get out of bed.

Above that space had been his bedroom. Here he had been a child, and here he had been forced to become a man. Or die.

He could still hear the soldiers abusing his mother and young love. It still made him feel sick. And angry. This is where revenge had become his single goal in life.

He sat stone faced amongst the wreckage of a neighbourhood, tears rolling unashamedly down his cheeks.

He was still fifteen.

"On the left you can see the National Museum, quite probably robbed of all things worth having, and on the right the Hospice Sulaymaniyah. Up ahead the tall, white coloured, overly modern skyscraper is our hotel," Lilia told them. "God knows what we'll find there, but it is home for the time being."

The two men stared ahead, watching a tall white building that seemed to grow out of a totally wooded area.

"Either side of the hotel are parks: to the left is Al Manshya Park and to the right is Al Jalaa' Park. The area is beautiful, and by the looks of it hasn't suffered too terribly so far."

"Who'd believe you were in the same city as they show on telly?" Pete said in wonder. "Looks like a holiday resort."

"I can see what you were saying about pre-conflict Damascus," Jack said.

They pulled up in front of the Four Seasons, wondering what was coming next. A suited concierge strolled through the doors and up to Pete's door, a couple of porters following him.

"Did we somehow turn off into the Ritz?" Pete asked.

"Shall we have your car parked?" asked the man in the suit. "All part of the service."

Pete handed over the keys and climbed out of the car, wondering if the weapons under the rear floor would be noticed.

"Can you have our stuff sent to our rooms please? Just the rucksacks. The rest can stay in the car tonight," Lilia told the porter. "It's been a long day."

"Of course madam."

They walked into the reception area and checked in, the bill already settled by someone in the UK. Obviously their film company.

"We'll have someone see you to your rooms," the receptionist told them.

"No need," said Jack. "We have nothing to carry and a bit of exploring will do us no harm."

"As you wish, Sir."

As they walked to the lifts, Pete whistled and commented, "Better than the places we stayed in London."

"Not too hard really," Lilia announced. "Welcome to my home."

After an early dinner, they went to their rooms. It had been a stressful day, and they decided to leave any exploring until the next one.

At ten o'clock Jack knocked on Lilia's door. She opened it, pulled him close and kissed him.

He returned the kiss, then gently pushed her away. "Business first. What do you think? Is it the way you expected?"

"Too soon to say," she told him, trying to find his kiss again. "It is a city that has survived invaders and coups for as long as it can remember. Why not survive this one?"

She took hold of his shoulders, pulling him closer. He half-succumbed but tried to complete his task. "Did you recognise the place? Did it feel safe?"

"I got us here didn't I?" she asked. "And now I'm with you. Of course I'm safe."

He gave in.

Chapter Fourteen

20th August 2013, Damascus, Syria

After a light breakfast, the group decided to go for a stroll in Al Jalaa' Park. It would be a chance to feel the city from outside of the vehicle and stretch their legs. Maybe meet some locals. Then Lilia could talk to people and learn a little more.

They crossed Brazil Avenue and entered the grassy grounds. Tall trees added to the already green area and gave the place a cool feeling compared to the barren mountains they'd left yesterday. It was strange to think that the land would turn into the Syrian desert not many miles from where they were now. Mountains, lush greenery, sand. A land of change.

The park was abandoned, but still appeared well kept. Bushes trimmed, grass short.

"We have parks all over the city," Lilia told them. "In the old days, the families would come here and picnic on weekends. I have many fond memories here." A far-away look was on her face as her mind drifted to better times.

They continued walking towards the north of the park, hearing only limited traffic on the surrounding roads.

"Sounds quiet out there," Jack said.

"These roads would normally be jammed with traffic at this hour," Lilia said. "Same as cities anywhere I guess, rush hour is rush hour. I guess business isn't too good right now."

They reached the top end of the park, the bushes denser to separate it from the avenue beyond.

Pete suddenly stepped forward, blocking the way from Lilia and Jack, his back to them. "Come out," he ordered. "We're friendly, but don't do anything stupid."

Nothing happened, and Jack and Lilia looked at each other, confused looks on their faces.

"Come on mate," Pete tried again. "I saw you."

The bushes rustled, then the outer branches were brushed aside. A boy of maybe ten years of age was there, appearing unwashed and wearing ripped and dirty clothes. He looked scared, but came towards Pete, who had taken an apple, that he'd got from the breakfast, out of his pocket.

"Here. It's yours."

The boy took the apple, at arms-length, still wary. Lilia came forward.

"Who are you?"

After a small frown of uncertainty, the boy appeared to make a conscious decision to trust them. Maybe the apple helped. Food was always good.

"I'm Jaf," he told them. "I live here in the bushes."

"Why do you live in the bushes Jaf? Where is your mum? Where's your house?"

"It was blown up. I lost mum. So I live here."

Lilia crouched down and took his hand. "Do you live alone?"

"No," he told them, looking over his shoulder to the undergrowth. "I live with some other boys who have no homes."

Pete was looking into the foliage, trying to see if anyone else was there. "Where are they now?"

"They go to work during the day and get us food. They say I'm too young for that, so I look after our stuff."

Lilia looked to Jack, a look that said she hoped he had an answer, a solution. He shook his head. "We'll come down later Jaf," he said. "We'll bring you some food. Do you have blankets and bedding?"

"We do. We got stuff from the houses that are damaged."

"When are the rest back here?"

"About middle of the afternoon."

"We'll come back then. Tell them to expect us and tell them we are friends. Tell them that we have come from England."

The team backed away, Lilia giving the boy a hug. He disappeared back into his bush.

After a coffee in the hotel reception area, they decided to have a look around the park on the other side of the hotel, Al Manshya. It was similar to Al Jalaa' but perhaps a little more unkempt. It's hard to find park-keepers in a war zone they concluded.

Exiting the far side of the park from the hotel they came upon their first problem. A two-man military check point and, unlike the day before, there was no way they could avoid it as it was right there.

"Papers please," the corporal requested in Arabic. Lilia took the passports from the bag.

"You speak Arabic, but you hold British passports?" he questioned. "Are you from here?"

Jack and Pete followed the exchange, not catching every word, but understanding enough. "Yes I am from here," Lilia informed the soldier. "But I lived in England. I have come back to try and let the world see what is happening here with my film crew."

The corporal eyed the two men suspiciously. He switched to English. "Where are your cameras?"

"We're just arrived yesterday, so we thought we would have a look around first," Lilia continued. "We want to show people how Damascus is still a safe place to come to, so first we need to know where there are good places to film."

The corporal eyed the passports, studying the visas. "These appear to be wrong," he told them. "I'm not sure if we can let you continue," he added, winking to the other soldier with him. Jack caught the gesture and guessed where things were going.

"Maybe we buy you a beer or two?" he said taking a twenty US dollar note out of his pocket. "You could tell us all about the city."

"Beer is costing much more than that nowadays," the corporal replied.

Jack added a second note. "Twenty for each of you," he said. "Should cover a drink after work."

The two notes disappeared inside the corporals pocket. "I'll let it go this time," he told them. "Maybe we could meet for a drink," he then said, to Lilia, in Arabic again. "I could show you around. Maybe have a little fun."

Lilia knew what he meant but played dumb. "Maybe after I finish the assignment for the company. Do you have a phone number?"

The corporal scribbled a number on a notebook page, ripped it out and passed it to Lilia.

"I'll be in touch," she said. They continued on their way.

Ahmed woke in the cellar room he called home. He knew it was after ten o'clock, but it had been a late night. He had been on a raid with a number of other boys on the instruction of one of the regional commanders. The rebel movement was becoming more organised now, and often attacks were planned to coincide with each other, one hitting a police station, one an army check point, another a government office. Apart from causing widespread chaos, it also split up the military reaction to the attacks, making it less efficient.

Normally the group only knew its own task, so if it was compromised it wouldn't affect the other missions that were going on. This sometimes also led to confusion, with rebel groups bumping in to one another and taking friendly casualties.

His Kalashnikov lay in the corner.

He rolled up his blanket, pulling on a dirty sweatshirt. He had half a water melon and a bottle of water in a small shoulder bag. Breakfast.

He pulled on his trainers and climbed the stairs through the pile of rubble to the outside world, carefully looking around before showing himself fully. Nothing. No-one. He clambered down the debris and sat in the sun, enjoying its soft rays. The summer was coming to its end, but the chill of winter hadn't set in yet. That would follow over the next couple of months.

He sat in the sun, relaxing while he recharged his batteries. Tonight would be another long one.

At just before five o'clock they were back in Al Jalaa' Park. Pete and Jack both had small rucksacks on their backs while Lilia carried a clear pack of six plastic water bottles, shrink-wrapped together. The sun was getting lower in the sky and the evening chill was just setting in.

Pete stopped them before they reached the bushes at the top end of the park.

"I'll go over alone and get them to move over to us in the open. These guys have lived rough for a while, and better we have some sort of control of the situation," he told them over his shoulder. "Just be a minute."

As he reached the bushes, Jaf stepped out.

"Hi Jaf," Pete said. "Are your friends back?"

Another boy emerged, maybe fourteen years of age. Then another, about the same. A tall lad — maybe six feet tall — came out. He had a baseball bat in his hand. "Who are you?" he asked.

"I'm an English guy who met Jaf this morning. We brought you some food."

"We have food."

"And you don't want more?" asked Pete, knowing the answer. "We're not here to hurt you or interfere with how you live. We just thought it would be good to give you some of the food we get from the hotel over there." He pointed towards the hotel. "Come over and get it if you're interested. If not, we'll just leave you alone." He turned and started towards the others.

The boys looked at one another, uncertain. "They were OK to me this morning," Jaf told them. "One of them is one of us, a Syrian lady."

Pete reached Jack and Lilia. "They're a bit suspicious," he said. "Might not come over."

Lilia looked towards the end of the park. The light was fading now and she wondered if this was such a good idea after all.

"We give them five more minutes and then go," Jack said. "Don't want to be around too long after dark."

Pete sat down next to the packs.

Three of the five minutes passed, and none of the boys showed. Then, out of a bush about sixty feet to their left, Jaf appeared. "Hi," he said. "The others are coming. They're just a little shy." He walked over and sat next to Pete.

Five more boys including the tall leader made their way forward. Jack emptied the food from the bags and put the water with it. They came and collected it but did not hang around.

"Bye," said Jaf, following the bigger lads back to the bush. "And thanks."

They watched him go, stood and turned back to the hotel.

"It's a bloody sad country when kids have to live like that," said Lilia. "I guess things can't get much worse than this."

Oh, but they could.

Chapter Fifteen

Early hours, 21st August 2013, Ghouta, Damascus, Syria

Mount Qasioun stands on the north side of Damascus, overlooking the city. It is not a monster of a mountain, standing at just over 3,775 feet at its highest point. It is steeped in religious history, relevant both to Christianity and Islamic faiths.

The Magharat al-Dam, so the story goes, is a cave where the first man Adam — a character found in both the Quran and the Bible — lived. It is also said to be the place where Cain killed Abel. The translation to English gives it the name 'The Cave of Blood' in remembrance of the murder that took place there.

Magharat al-Ju — the Cave of Famine— is another religious spot where, some say, forty saints died from starvation. Others say it was forty prophets.

Another famous cave on the mountain was the place where seven Christians were sent by the Romans. They were requested to review their belief in Jesus and take up Rome's values. When they failed to do this, the authorities boarded up the mouth of the cave when the men were asleep, only for them to waken up 180 years later. These 'Seven Sleepers' also feature in the Quran, but here they are referred to as 'The People of the Cave.'

In the early hours of the morning on the 21st August, Colonel Habil al-Shaar sat in his command vehicle, three mobile multi-tube rocket launchers to his rear near the summit of the mountain. He silently considered what he was about to do.

Launching the rockets on fellow Syrians was not making him feel good. The only thing that made it seem more acceptable was the knowledge that many of the enemy assembled against him were not actually from Syria. He knew that Iraqis, Iranians, Pakistanis, even Americans and English were down there fighting with the rebels and destroying his beautiful country. He just wished they would all go home, and that Damascus could go back to where it had been. He knew his President wasn't perfect, but under him he had done very well and the country had been stable. Now it was a mess.

A sergeant put his head through the open window on the other side of the jeep. "Everything is checked, Sir. We can launch whenever you're ready."

He took a deep breath, released it slowly, turning to the NCO. "Thanks Sarge. Give me a minute to make a call."

Picking up the cell phone from the dashboard, he flicked through his contacts list, selecting a number he didn't use too often.

"Yes General, al-Shaar here. We are ready to launch."

To the south and east of Damascus is the agricultural area of Ghouta. The farms here grow wheat and barley, maize and alfalfa, and fruit trees supply plums and walnuts. It is a belt of green around the city before turning to dry grasslands and eventually the Syrian Desert. In Spring it is a popular area for city residents to escape to, but at this time of the year it is really only the locals who are around. The area was controlled by those opposed to the Assad regime.

The towns and villages in the region to the east of the city — Markaz Rif Dimashq district, places such as Jisrayn, Siqba, Hammurah — were just coming to life for another day. Early starters made their way to work in the city, kids were fed breakfast, people moved to the farms where they would work the fields. The sun was on the slow rise.

As a rebel stronghold, fighting with the Assad military was not unusual, and shelling of the area was frequent, but often ineffective. Fields don't die.

The first rockets from Mount Qasioun hit the villages at around five in the morning. The shelling only went on for fifteen minutes as the three launchers cleared their tubes, reloaded and cleared them once more.

It was just another attack on the rebels.

But something was different. These rockets didn't explode with the same effect as usual. They still killed whoever they hit, but they didn't have the same explosive force.

When the shelling ceased, the survivors came out of their shelters. At first all was as usual: wrecked buildings, smoke, some small fires. After a short while though, all of that changed.

Jamil coughed, rubbed his eyes. Coughed again. "You OK?" asked his wife Aini. She had just left the shelter of the house. He coughed again.

"Just the smoke from the shells I guess," he told her, another cough.

Their three-year-old daughter Judi came out. She was rubbing her eyes. Spluttering into her hand.

Kalila, a neighbour from the next house came out. She was coughing and carrying her son Hana. "He's not breathing properly," she cried. "I can't get him to breathe."

Suddenly Jamil threw up his entire stomach contents, falling to his knees in the process. He was dry-heaving, nothing left to come up. Aini moved across to him to help, but just then Judi did the same thing.

Another child – Nawwar – crawled out of the house of Kalila, also being sick, blood noticeable in the discharge.

Jamil was now lying on the ground, moaning and hardly moving. He rubbed his eyes. His wife was trying to help her daughter Judi, but now she too was starting to cough violently. Jamil had now lost consciousness, lying still in his own vomit. His wife fell next to him, no longer able to help her young girl who was vomiting uncontrollably. Aini was sick, weak, scratching at her eyes.

The scene was being repeated all over the village and in a few surrounding places where the rockets had struck. People were going down like flies.

It would take only a few hours for people to know this had been a chemical attack, and not the first in the conflict. It would take longer before the accusation would surface saying it was the nerve agent Sarin, and it would take a couple of weeks before the United Nations inspection team were able to confirm it. The UN Secretary General, Ban Ki-Moon, would label it as a War Crime.

Syria had just sunk to a new low.

The Four Seasons Hotel suddenly became a hive of activity: cars arriving at all hours with camera crews; UN inspectors arriving with specialist equipment for testing and identifying chemicals; the world press hoping to get a look at the piles of bodies out at Ghouta.

Everybody expected the Americans to leap into the fray with both feet. It was their normal response to this kind of thing: act first, consider later.

The politicians were having a whale of a time, in the US, all the European majors, in the Middle East. First opinion was that the attack had to be from the Assad people. The grade of Sarin used was high: too good to be easily accessible, and the rebels didn't have the delivery systems to deliver such an attack, never mind carrying it out on their own people. But Bashar al-Assad hadn't survived as long as he had without having a fight in him: he immediately blamed the rebels, accusing them of killing their own and trying to turn world opinion against him. He received the backing of the Russians and, to a slightly lesser extent, the Chinese. This slowed down the USA's knee-jerk reaction. Maybe it stopped an all-out Arab regional war.

At breakfast, Jack and the others tried to get a handle on things. Rumours were rife, but facts very thin on the ground. Lilia listened to the babble of Arab voices and tried to translate the stories.

"Some sort of rocket attack a couple of hours ago," she told the men. "People in the farming region off to the east. A lot of people getting sick." She stopped as a woman, in her black burka, hit the table, spilling an orange juice. "She says they've gone too far this time. Killed hundreds. Women and children rather than rebel fighters."

Jack was eavesdropping further up the table, his Arabic not keeping up with the story. "Are they saying it was a chemical weapon attack?" he asked. "I think that's what I picked up."

Lilia listened for about thirty seconds. "You're right. That's what they believe. The UN has asked to send observers to the area, but right now the regime is blocking them. They expect more people to be here this evening, ready to go."

"How does this affect us?" Pete asked. "Are they restricting movement?"

"Could work in our favour," Jack said. "If the world press pour in, we can just join the hordes and get around the city a little easier."

"Always a silver lining," Pete said softly. "Except for the poor bastards out there."

"God bless them," Lilia whispered. "And give them strength."

The truth was probably never going to be known but, in the coming days, an estimated seventeen hundred were reported to have died. Bodies were piled up in mass graves and children laid out in halls and mortuaries, to allow devastated parents to identify their offspring. Hundreds of them to be named.

If the parents had survived.

The UN inspectors found positive evidence of Sarin in urine, hair and blood samples. They found parts of rockets that indicated the type of delivery system. They saw the mass graves.

But no-one accepted liability.

Syria was turning into a very dirty war. It had to stop.

Chapter Sixteen

23rd August 2013, Damascus, Syria

It was ten o'clock at night, the light had long gone and the part of the city Ahmed was in was quiet, except for the silent whispers of the rebels waiting to be led. They were an angry squad of soldiers, still not believing what had happened two days before in Ghouta. Many had lost friends and family in the attacks. It hurt.

Ahmed had his own small group of eight rebels. They sat around in the rubble cleaning their weapons. Tonight though, his was just part of a bigger gathering, instead of being a squad-sized attack tonight, the rebel leaders had planned something more on platoon scale, dragging in many smaller bands of men.

They were planning a 'spectacular', a hit that would hurt the Assad military the way the rockets had hurt them.

Each squad leader was called forward to a more senior member of the rebel council. He was asked about how many troops he had, the make-up of their weaponry and how much ammunition each man carried. The results were then recorded and discussed by a group of senior officers, a plan put together. More weapons and ammo that had been hidden in caches throughout the city were then distributed amongst the less well-equipped teams. Team leaders were then brought together.

The senior officer stepped forward and sat down amongst the men.

"The whore known as Assad inflicted great casualties on our people two days back. People are still dying and suffering from the effects of the chemical weapons launched against innocent Syrians in the Ghouta region. Many people here amongst us lost loved ones, friends, brothers and sisters, in the attack. We may never know how many of our people died in the past days."

He was forty-five years old, a former university lecturer. He shifted his position, his legs crossed awkwardly under him, unused to such discomfort.

"I am not a fighting man, and nor are most of you in front of me. We have all been forced to fight, and we will need the experience you have all gained from the fighting to hurt our enemies. Some of you were with the Syrian Army and have left to join your band of brothers. We need you to continue to teach us, to improve our skills. To lead us wisely.

"Tonight we will avenge those who suffered at Ghouta. I have a plan."

Colonel Habil al-Shaar looked down at the city of Damascus. In the old days, the whole area would have flickered with house lights, street lights. Beams of car headlights would have carved through the darkness, looking like fireflies from up here on the mountain. Now vast areas of the city stood in blackness, the electrical infrastructure of that area destroyed in the fighting. Curfew meant few vehicles moved around. People — unlit and — moved down there, both hostile and friendly. It was good to be high on the slopes of Mount Qasioun and far away from the fear and anger of the streets and houses that crouched below him.

It was just after midnight and he thought he would turn in shortly. A last walk along the positions, a few words to inspire the men on guard duty, tasked with the night's security. The air was cool and fresh, and he wondered if sleep would come quickly once he was down. He had seen the results of his bombardment on TV, even though the local stations tried to hide it. Social media meant the devastation had been passed to a worldwide audience. His men viewed it on their cell phones, whispered about it, probably as sickened by it as he was, but fearful of saying this out loud.

The regime was still strong.

"Evening Sergeant, any problems?" he asked as he entered the Operations Room.

"All quiet Sir," the NCO replied, shocked to see the Colonel still about. "No reports of any fighting in the city tonight. Seems to be all calm right now."

A calm before the storm, as the British put it, he thought, careful not to voice this.

"Good news. I'll be turning in shortly. Just a quick walk around the launchers."

"Goodnight, Sir."

He left the warmth of the Ops and walked over to the nearest mobile rocket launcher. A Private sat in the driver's seat, keeping himself warm. He hurriedly leapt out when he saw Al-Shaar.

"Relax soldier, just checking everything's good here," the Colonel told him.

"Nothing to report, Sir. All quiet. I'll be doing some maintenance on the vehicle shortly. Just thought I'd warm up a bit first," the Private gushed out.

Al-Shaar continued on until he came to the next lorry, the launch tubes on the back a black area even against the deep darkness of the mountain. He thought about the deadly cargo he had ordered them to discharge two days before. He shivered, and not because of the cold.

Completing his tour, he went to his bed. Sleep was elusive.

They'd been split into groups, approximately fifteen men in each one, and the university man had assigned targets to each team. He had told them that the Ghouta strike had originated from Mount Qasioun, and they all knew that this was a stronghold for the Assad military. Somehow this professor had a fair idea of the layout of the rocket battery on the mountain. He also had information that this was the source of the attack. How he knew, no-one asked.

They had walked for over an hour to get to the lower slopes of the hill, still in the shelter of housing, some of it empty, after fighting. The professor seemed to have the quieter areas mapped in his head.

Passing through the area of Al Mouhajrin, just below the mountain and at a point where the best viewing points had been in the days of peace, the rebels could see the horrible levels of destruction that had fallen on the streets there. It seemed that not one house or flat was undamaged. Gaping holes opened the sides of buildings where shells had passed straight through. Structural steelwork hung from the tops of flats where the upper floors had once been, twisted and bent, looking like some sort of modern art gone wrong.

Yet they knew people still lived there, unbelievable though this should have been. They all lived in wrecks of what were once homes, so they understood that life did go on despite the outward appearance of the houses.

They reached the edge of the built-up area. The university man moved forward, calling a couple of his lieutenants up to him.

"The troops are mainly a little over to the right, and our targets are only about halfway up the hill. I know a ravine that we can follow part way up – I used it myself when I carried out my reconnaissance. It's almost one o'clock now, so they should be down to minimum manning and most switched off. They will have night-vision equipment, but if they feel no threat, they probably aren't using it continuously."

One of the men with him was using a night-scope. "I can see men up there, but not many. A sentry walking around perhaps, and a couple in fixed positions."

"As I explained when we started, I believe they have three mobile launchers on the road up there. One group must take these out. This is more for show than anything else: they have plenty more, but it's a sort of justice for our people. For the folk of Ghouta. We'll hit the lorries with the RPGs."

He nodded to the young man leading this attack.

"The second group will take out the command post." He pointed to a second man. "That's your task. It also has the sleeping quarters for those off duty. Take them out too."

The third man who'd been using the night vision equipment looked at the teacher. "And me?" he asked.

"We need something big, something the whole city can see. We need to put ourselves back on the map."

"I have thirteen men with guns and explosives. Not quite an army. Any suggestions?"

"I have."

The Colonel couldn't sleep. It had been the same the previous night too, images of children and women choking to death on their own vomit, babies scratching at their eyes to try and stop the irritation, men unable to breath or to help their families. There had also been pictures of the farm animals heaped onto piles, stiff, as rigor mortis had set in. He wondered if the chemicals would also have an effect on the already useless water table out there: no water, no crops, the animals dead and no-one to work the land. What had they done?

He had been in the Syrian Army all of his life. A spell in the UK at Sandhurst Military Academy as he'd once been a promising young recruit, but now he had over twenty-five years of service. In all of that time he had never felt so guilty of abusing his power. Disgusted with himself and his uniform.

He got up and poured himself a coffee in a small cup, black, two sugars and no milk.

The first two groups were near the top of the channel that ran up the mountain. The professor was slightly behind and in contact with a man at the bottom of the mountain who watched the ascent through the night vision goggles, checking ahead for signs of their enemy. They would soon reach the place where the ravine ran under the road, and here the two groups would split.

The university man let his mind drift for a moment, wondering where he would be if this war had never happened. Probably in his bed now, maybe with a young student, teaching her practical biology instead of Arab history that he specialised in.

He pulled his mind back to the present. The advance troops were at the bridge.

The lead soldier checked that the coast was clear and then the first group filtered along the road to the right of the wadi, to where they were told they would find the launchers. They kept to the side of the road where the mountain sloped upwards, trying to blend better with the darkness of the rocks, not silhouetting themselves from below. The second group continued up the hill towards the site of the command post and living quarters.

About two hundred yards later the lead group saw the shape of the launcher trucks on the road ahead. Still no sign of the military, they moved off the road and prepared the RPGs. Two RPGs were sighted against each lorry, with the rest of the team providing all around defence. They now waited for group two to start their attack.

The second group were also on their target, their leader fanning them out and assigning targets with a point of the finger, first at the soldier he wanted to use, then at the target the man should attack. A final questioning open-handed expression to all of them and all returned an affirmative nod. They were ready to go.

The Lieutenant gave the signal and all rose, running towards the enemy positions, yelling at the top of their voices.

The Colonel heard the shouts coming from outside the accommodation and feared the worst. He was barefoot, heading for the window, taking a revolver as he went and wishing he had something more substantial.

As he reached the window, the door flew open, smashing back against its hinges with a bang, filling with the shape of a man. His head moved in the direction of the intruder, his shooting arm following instinctively, body following that. The first round was fired even before the arm was parallel with the ground, hitting the soldier in the lower leg and spinning him round, knocking him down, his bellow turning into a tortured scream. The Colonel fired again at the body mass, moving towards the back of the room where he could take some cover from behind a metal cupboard.

A second man hurdled over the first, machine gun blazing inaccurately from the waist. The officer fired again, but on the move and under stress, the bullet going high and wide. Another burst from the AK47 took the colonel across the chest and he went down, dead before his body hit the floor.

Hearing the gunfire from above them, the RPG shooters prepared their weapons. From the furthest launcher, a man leapt from the truck cabin, looking in the direction of the shooting. Another appeared from around the back of the middle lorry, looking across to his colleague to see if he had an explanation.

"Fire!" the rebel commander shouted.

Within the space of a second, all six grenade launchers spewed their projectiles towards their designated targets. The riflemen opened up on the unlucky drivers.

Many of the government troops were asleep in their beds as the attack began, not having had any chance to retaliate before the rebels were in the dormitories. Many died in their beds, some got out naked and were gunned down before they reached either their weapons or their clothes.

A grenade was lobbed into the command post, and after the crunch of the explosion, smoke poured out of the shattered door. Rebels came in, guns blazing.

A machine gun emplacement behind the post opened up, finally returning some fire and taking down two of the rebel soldiers. One died instantly, the other lay on the ground, moaning and in shock, his intestines hanging out of his stomach cavity where the rounds had exited him. A grenade was hurled towards the gun post, temporarily hushing it, until a new gunner took charge.

In the chaos, one of the rebels shot his colleague as he came towards him through thick smoke.

Another grenade landed directly in the machine gun post, and the battle was largely over, the rebels simply moving around and silencing the still-living enemy.

Down below the mountain, the Syrian Army was trying desperately to find out what was going on above their heads. The sound of gunfire and explosions was clear on the still night air, but communications with the command post were lost. Radio operators repeated calls to the position, but nothing came back over the ether.

"Get the armour over here now!" a Captain bellowed. His infantry men were armed and ready to go, only waiting for armoured personnel carriers to whisk them up the mountain. There was a nervous tension amongst the soldiers, a knowledge that fellow fighters were in trouble.

An APC rolled into the yard, a cleared area in the middle of a wrecked neighbourhood. Another followed. Troops tried to board.

"We need to fuel these two up before we go," the commander called from the turret. "The others will be here shortly and they are already full."

The two machines moved to the rear of the area, where large rubber fuel tanks were propped in place with rubble and sandbags. There were four tanks, leaving room to fill four APCs at a time, in line, so large was the fuel dump, each black rubber tank containing over 20,000 gallons of diesel. Rear echelon troops rolled out filling nozzles and connected up the APCs.

Other APCs rolled in to the yard and started boarding the waiting soldiers, engines roaring.

Group three of the rebel forces were watching the fuel dump from about half a football pitch distance. The activity and the noise were just what they wanted, and their commander gave the order to move covertly forward to the rear side of the fuel tanks. Here half of the group started unpacking Bergens as the rest covered them, in all around defence.

From out of the packs came plastic explosives, detonators and firing mechanisms. The explosives were packed between the rubber of the bladder tank and the rocks that propped them up. The rebels had no real explosives training, just trial and error experience, but they knew that if something expanded at high speed, it would take the easiest route to relieve the pressure it created. Rubber was softer than rock, so the tank would be the loser as the explosive blast tried to escape.

Detonators came next, forced by fingers into the pale plastic charge, the wires sealed in place as the men worked the explosive like it was putty. Wires were attached on hardboard thimbles, then the force began to withdraw, back to the damaged building line, trailing the wire behind them.

At a safe hundred and fifty feet, they positioned themselves behind walls that still seemed sound and had a rubble buffer in front of them. They connected the firing devices.

With the roar of the approaching APCs, the two teams on the mountain started their way down the hillside, far from the roads. Searchlights carved up the ground from the safety of the bases at the foot of the hill, but it was a guessing game as to where the rebels were or might be.

In the darkness it was easy to twist an ankle on the rocky ground but staying on the road meant either capture or death, or one followed soon after by the other.

They hurried downwards, knowing they needed to reach the safety of the destroyed townships as soon as possible in order to stay alive.

The first APC was refuelled and moving away from the fuel bladder tanks. Another one pulled into the yard and started loading troops. A tank of dubious vintage pulled into the yard, heavy wood panels hanging off the sides to help the armour to repel rocket propelled grenades launched towards the occupants. It crossed to the rear and pulled over to refuel.

Hatch already open, the driver stood back from the controls and yelled to the fuel handler. "Need to fill it up."

The driver climbed onto the deck and made his way to the rear to help.

It was the last act he ever carried out.

The wires were now all connected to the firing mechanisms. The whole team pressed their bodies into the ground. The signal was given. The operators pressed the buttons, eyes closed.

On the slopes of the mountain the darkness became light. The blasts all came roughly together, a great boom of noise shaking the earth, flames soaring into the night sky. The fuel in the bladder tanks caught on, adding to the blaze, the whole city hearing and seeing the result.

People close to the tanks died instantly, others were drenched in burning fuel, their screams masked by the noise coming from the blaze and the resulting deafness of the explosion. Looking from the shelter of the buildings, they were like small matches, running flames, before collapsing in agony.

The armoured personnel carrier and the tank still connected to the inferno that had once been a fuel storage tank also burned. Ammunition in the vehicles cooked off in the vast heat and exploded, the tank shells ripping the hull to pieces and throwing shrapnel in every direction. Stray rounds from the vehicles scythed through the air, but no bodies were still standing to stop them.

Some of the rebels were caught on the slopes in the half-light from the blaze. Lucky for most of them the government troops had other things on their minds, but some professional soldiers shot at the tail-enders, causing more death.

Looking from the city, the slopes of Mount Qasioun were speckled with fire from the burning launchers, the command post and living accommodation. Added to this, the massive fire, in the buildings close by, lit the sky and the lower slopes.

It looked like the demons from the infamous caves of the mountain had been released again…

It was five o'clock in the morning when Ahmed reached home and crawled into his pile of rubble. He was exhausted, having led his squad back through a city of sirens, fires and tanks. His original team of eight soldiers was reduced to one of only five.

He rolled out his sleeping bag, drank some lukewarm water, and was asleep before his head hit the concrete.

Chapter Seventeen

24th August 2013, Four Seasons Hotel, Damascus, Syria

The team had been stuck in the hotel for three days now and a touch of cabin fever was setting in. The reports were trickling back, following the chemical attack, but the Assad administration was still blocking the inspectors from visiting the site to gain first-hand information. The full story was sketchy at best, with casualty figures changing hourly.

Then in the early hours of the morning they'd all been awakened with the firework show at Mount Quasioun. As yet, there were no reports as to what had happened there. Again the government was controlling the media.

"Has anybody heard what was going on last night yet?" asked Jack, as he joined Pete and Lilia at breakfast. He looked tired from being up half of the night, but the shower had helped a little.

"Nothing new," said Lilia. "The hotel staff are advising people to stay indoors. The military are putting on a bit of a show-of-force right now, tanks and armoured cars charging around everywhere."

"We're guessing it was the rebels giving Assad's lot grief, but no-one is sure," Pete added. "Now with the increased military presence it looks like they'll try and nail the rebels."

Lilia swallowed a mouthful of croissant. "The guy on the door this morning told me that the army has a bit of a stronghold over by the mountain. Vehicles and manpower. It seems that there's a bit of tit-for-tat going on after the chemical thing."

"Makes sense," said Jack attacking a chicken sausage. "They'll be hurting if the reports are true. A lot of normal people must have lost family during that one."

The waiter came around with the coffee refills. They sat and ate silently for a few minutes.

"So what do we do?" Lilia asked. "Sit here, or get out and try and make something happen?"

Jack knew she'd had once had many friends in Damascus. Not knowing if they were still alive must have been killing her inside. So close to them, but so far.

"It'll be quite dangerous out there right now," Pete warned. "And if everyone else is staying inside, then we stick out like a sore thumb. Plus the troops will be nervous, trigger happy."

"When the press corps start venturing out again, then so do we," Jack said.

They looked around the breakfast room, noting it was fuller than usual with hacks and United Nations personnel. Neither the UN inspection teams nor the press corps were getting out either. Both Pete and Jack were right.

"I feel so bloody useless," Lilia stormed. "I'm going to my room."

Jack was on a secure mobile phone that the team in the UK had issued them before they left for the Middle East. He was talking to Colin in Beirut, leaving the restaurant to take the call.

"Information from London is very uncertain right now," Colin was saying into a matching secure-speech handset.

"The chemicals are down to Assad though?" Jack asked.

"It certainly looks that way. The rebels just don't have that type of equipment — launchers and rockets — available to them, never mind access to chemical weapons. You've also got to keep in mind that the people who could supply this — the Russians for example — are actually not on the side of the rebels. We know Assad had a chemical capability before this all kicked off. It's just that no-one thought he'd be mad enough to use it."

Jack nodded in agreement, even though Colin couldn't see him. "And the fireworks display a couple of nights later?"

"The rebels are claiming that. A spokesman in Lebanon has said it was a fuel dump they hit, plus they claim they destroyed the launcher trucks used in the Ghouta attack." Colin waited a second for a response, and when none came added, "Of course no-one can verify this so far."

"It makes sense," Jack told him. "Talking to locals, the government troops had a stronghold in that area, and where better to launch a missile strike from than halfway up a mountain."

Another short silence. "Jack, people back home wonder if you should still be there right now. Could be the hotel next. A place full of foreigners would make a great high-visibility target. All over the papers if that happened."

"We thought about that, but do you think anyone would do something so stupid with the UN camped out here too?"

"Did you think they would launch a chemical attack against their own people? These people are not too rational it would seem."

"We stay," Jack replied. "We've discussed it and we stay." He had his back to the wall so he could make sure no-one was coming too close and eavesdropping. No-one was within about sixty-five feet of him, so safe so far. "I think we are safer in the hotel than outside it for now. Let's give it another day or two and then reassess the situation."

"You're the man on the ground," Colin said. "Good luck."

Ahmed sat silently in the wreckage of the house, listening for sounds of soldiers or tanks. After five minutes of nothing, he raised his head until his eyes could see the land surrounding the bombed-out house. Nothing and no-one.

The hours following the attack on Mount Quasioun had been spent in hiding. The Assad forces had flooded the city, tanks and armoured cars everywhere, but troops mainly staying mounted in the vehicles. Helicopters had flown overhead, looking for signs of rebel gatherings, and once he'd seen a pair of fighter jets come in from the north and bomb an area known to be held by rebels.

It was not a time to go roaming the streets, but Ahmed wanted to find out what was going on.

Climbing down from the pile of rubble, he crossed the street to what had once been a block of flats. Sections of the building were missing, no windows contained any glass anymore, and most of the doors were gone. Black stains on the walls showed where fires had burned as a car was torched, or a flat was burnt out. This estate had once been filled with buildings like this, and some were still semi-inhabitable, some totally flattened. Over a thousand people had once lived in this small area, now all gone.

Using the flats for cover, he moved through the first block, exiting it and running over to the next building. These routes were the new roadways in the city. Hidden within the building meant you could transit from point-to-point without walking in the open. Fighters used the buildings to set-up ambushes for the government troops, waiting for them to come by on foot patrol, shooting one or two, then using the same routes to escape the area.

He crossed another gap between blocks, taking as little time as possible in the open.

Twenty cautious minutes later, he arrived at his destination. Deep in one of the blocks, a set of stairs descended to a cellar area. The whole block was a mess, walls collapsed, broken furniture mixed with the debris. If you didn't know where the steps were, then you'd be very lucky to find them.

Having a final look around to make sure he wasn't watched, he headed down into the cellar.

"London think we should come out," he told Pete and Lilia. "They worry about the safety of the hotel, whether one of the sides might decide to use it to grab the newspapers with a spectacular. I told them I thought it was the safest place we could be right now."

They were in Jack's room, Lilia in a pair of jeans and lilac green open neck blouse, Pete in a pair of khaki shorts and a black T-shirt. Lilia had very little make-up on and looked as if she hadn't slept too well. Both the men now knew that she'd also once had friends living in the Ghouta region and that she was worried that they had remained there even after the war had started. The worst thing for her was that there was absolutely no way to find out, one way or the other.

"We can't leave," she said simply. "That is giving in to the bastard."

Jack looked at her, a little shocked at the venom in her voice. He said nothing, just letting it ride and glancing at Pete, communicating with his eyes that he should just leave it.

"I agree with Jack," said Pete. "With the place full of UN inspectors, press and the likes, here is as safe as anywhere in Damascus."

"So at least we all agree on that one," Jack concluded. He smiled at them both, trying to lighten the mood. "I thought we should try and make a plan as to what we do once things calm down a bit. You know, a bit of a brainstorming session."

"Kill Assad and save my bloody country," Lilia said in a low voice. She didn't even lift her eyes to look at them as she spoke. Pete looked nervously to Jack.

"Lilia," Jack said softly, his face giving nothing away as to his feelings. "I know…we both know… that this is a horrible time for you right now. These are your countrymen. But we cannot lose our focus. We want what you want, but we must plan a way to do it that allows us all to survive this."

Lilia stood up, her face flushed. "I'll kill him myself," she said softly. "I do not need you two." She turned from them, heading for the door, slamming it as she left. The two men looked towards it.

Pete let out a long, frustrated sigh. "Shit!"

Jack looked from the still-rattling door to the young soldier. "Give her some space. She's having a tough time right now. Remember she is a civilian. We are more used to the waiting game." |

"I hope I never have to tell her that…"

In the cellar were six other men, only one as young as Ahmed, but none over forty. All of them were commanders of small rebel units, and here was where they came to be assigned a new target, a new task. They were all dirty, all tired and their clothes were falling to pieces. They all had a weapon with them, the condition of it like a badge of rank between them. The best of them had rifles and machine pistols captured during fighting or liberated from dead soldiers, the less lucky had weapons handed down from their parents and grandparents.

They looked to the stairs as footfalls were heard. One man in his mid-forties came down the steps, his own weapon hanging from his right shoulder.

"Hello brothers," he said. "Thanks for coming, and especially thanks for the other night. The enemy is still not sleeping well after that little adventure."

The men laughed and formed a circle around him, all pulling up a mismatched piece of furniture to sit on, chairs that had survived in the wreckage of one of the flats that had made up the block.

"So, let's see who we have left from Mount Quasioun. Then we can decide on the next strike."

In her room, Lilia looked down on the city. From the fifth floor she could see far over the local area, the flattened houses and flats, the burnt out cars and buses, the odd military vehicle that the rebels had beaten. The whole place was wasted, her people fleeing for the borders, and this was only one city. Before coming to Syria, reports from Aleppo, Homs and Hamah all told the same tales of destruction on a mass scale, people dying, people leaving, and people fighting.

She thought about her former friends that may even now be surviving in the wreckage of the city. Many could be dead. Many could be living in the camps on the borders, worrying even now about how to survive the coming winter, how to put their lives back together. Some would have joined the rebels.

She wanted to do the latter, even if it cost her everything. She felt a lot for Jack and the bond they had formed but sitting and watching was no longer an option. She couldn't wait anymore.

Ghouta had been the final straw.

Somehow she had to get out there and help. She knew that the men would not understand this, so she also knew she couldn't tell them.

She took out a bag and began deciding what to take with her. It couldn't be much.

Jack knocked on her door two hours later. No response. He rapped again, not too loud in case she was already asleep.

'Probably watching me through the spy-hole' he thought. He'd guessed she would not want to talk to him, but thought it was worth a try at least. He tried to look through the hole to see if he could detect movement, but only saw darkness.

"Lilia?" he said quietly. Nothing.

He went to his own room, deciding that morning would be soon enough to talk.

Chapter Eighteen

Late, 24th August 2013, Downtown Damascus, Syria

She wore the same jeans and the same green blouse as earlier, a light-weight pullover and a waterproof jacket the added items plus a small tote bag. She had a pair of Asics training shoes on her feet. Her hair was pulled under a baseball hat, trying to look less female than she actually was. The anger was gone from the night before, but the need to act was still hot in her mind. Sitting waiting was not an option.

Going straight into the park, she finally wondered if what she was doing was a little crazy: a single woman out alone in a city at war.

She made her way to the rear of the park again, hoping Jaf would be there. At first there was no-one, so she softly called his name. No reply. Nerves kicked in, her resolve fading.

Lilia thought about returning to the hotel.

A sound behind her, then a head appeared. It was Jaf. "Is that you lady?"

"Call me Lilia, but yes it is. Can we talk?"

"Did you bring food?"

She took a loaf of bread and a plastic bag containing some meat from out of the waterproof jacket and passed it to him. "It's not much, but here." Another of the lads came out of the bush and again she wondered if she was pushing her luck a little too far. "Are the others awake?"

"I'm sure they are by now," Jaf told her. She sat on the grass next to him. The rest of the boys wondered out, half asleep, unsure why she was there.

"I guess you are asking yourselves why I am here," she started. "I am a reporter, and I'd like to meet with the real rebel troops, make a movie supporting them from the propaganda that the government is putting on TV. Do you know how I could meet someone from them?"

They were walking through broken down buildings, along roads where the military had piled rubble at either end to stop vehicles using them. People's lives lay all around her: the broken doll a child had lost when a tank shell had destroyed her house and her innocence; superman pillows from a bed that was used as firewood; a picture of a happy smiling couple on their wedding day, one or both possibly dead by now; a pair of trousers, stained with blood. All viewed by the cone of light from the one torch the boys carried between them.

It seemed to Lilia that more houses were collapsed than standing. She wondered where all of the people had gone, then remembered her thoughts in the hotel – they were probably in a refugee camp in Lebanon, Turkey or Iran.

The boys stopped from time-to-time, making her take shelter while they checked the route ahead, or searched a newly deserted building for useful items. They were scruffy, and even the smallest things seemed to be of interest to them. Food was the number one though. Their youth was being stolen from them.

She wasn't certain where in the town they were anymore, the streets all looked similar and the road signs were a thing of the past, flattened by shell fire, tanks and buildings. She also realised it had been years since she'd lived here. England had become her home.

They'd walked an hour and fifteen minutes and the boys had halted again. Jaf took her hand and led her to the side again, out of sight of the road, behind some rubble.

It was coming up to four in the morning, the light just showing on the horizon in the east. A strange peacefulness settled over the city, a silent beauty, a space between the war and the peace, the dark and the light.

"When will our city be like it was before?" Jaf asked with the innocence of a child.

Lilia looked hard at him, wondering if this was the same person who had led her through a dark war-torn landscape for the last hour and odd. He sounded so vulnerable and young. It made her feel physically sick that she couldn't just do something to take Syria back in time.

"It will one day Jaf. I promise."

His eyes frowned, but the doubt didn't reach all the way to his face. She knew he didn't believe her, but also was sure that he wanted to. Something to cling to.

One of the lads came back across to them. "We need to move on. It will be light soon, and we need her off the street before then."

"How much farther?" she asked.

"Not more than twenty minutes."

They moved off again, walking a little quicker as the light grew in the sky. She was surprised at how fast the smaller boys could move.

After about fifteen minutes of marching at speed she was again taken aside. The larger boy came to her. "I will go and see my contact and hope he is willing to meet you. Otherwise we have to lie up all day to avoid the troops." He looked at Jaf. "Wait here. If I don't come back in ten minutes, you know what to do."

He was gone. She tried to make small talk, but the youths just made themselves comfortable where they lay and slept. Something she couldn't manage. Jaf looked out for danger.

It was light now and nothing hid the destruction of the surroundings. She wondered what would happen if they refused to meet her. Staying out in this wilderness until nightfall. If the wrong people found her she could guess the result. Abuse, beating and death. Maybe death would be her wish if things got really bad…

She jerked awake, surprising herself. She had dozed off too, slipping out of the real world and into a dream of life in Britain, cutting flowers from her garden, baking bread, sipping wine on the decking at the rear of her house. Somehow the escape to heaven just made her grasp how horrible this hell called Damascus had become. She glanced at the boys who all slept now — even Jaf — and tried to do the same, but sleep had gone for now, the realities of the surroundings crowding in.

"Let's go," a voice broke in. She'd dozed off again, but this time no dream. The other boys were on their feet and she got up, a little unbalanced. The voice had come from the big boy.

Sixty feet later he turned to the rest. "Stay here. Me and her go inside, but you fellas watch for the troops. You know the signals."

They went towards a pile of rubble, Lilia vaguely confused.

Ahmed sat in his bunker, wondering what the boys were bringing to him, but feeling in some way proud that they thought he was the right one to bring such a problem to. He had just turned fifteen, still a youth himself, but with almost two years of fighting under his belt and his own small team of soldiers. He was seen as a leader, whilst at the same time, not too old for the young to feel alienated. He was a sort of link between them and the senior figures in the resistance.

He heard someone scrabbling up the side of the rubble pile, reached for his weapon — an automatic reaction after all this time — then placed it beside him, hand on the handle behind the trigger. Firing an AK inside the room would be deafening.

A woman came down the steps, the boy waiting at the top. Even in the dim light, Ahmed could see she was striking — beautiful even — and maybe thirty years of age. Something in her poise reminded him of his Saumaya, a memory from another planet. He pushed the thought out of his brain.

He waved the boy out, asking him to keep watch with his team. He stood.

"Hello, my name is Ahmed."

"I am Lilia," she replied. "I hope you can help me."

Ahmed gave her a puzzled look. "You want me to help you? A journalist from Europe? You know how dangerous it is here?" A deep frown was on his face.

"I know. And I am not really a journalist, but I do want to do something for Syria, my home. I hoped you could help there. I would like to join your group."

"You know we lose people every night here? You know that they will rape and kill you if you're caught, as they did my mother and the woman who would have, one day, been my wife?" He paused, the anger leaving him. "This is no place for women."

Lilia felt as if she'd been slapped. So forward, so harsh, so young. She pushed on. "They also killed my husband, so I feel the pain too. It is not yours alone."

It was the young man's turn to feel chastised. He blushed and she could tell then that he was holding a position far beyond his years. She felt guilt. They were born from the same pain.

"I'm sorry. I didn't mean to attack you," she said.

He was looking down at the dusty floor between his crossed legs, contemplating what to say. No-one said anything for sixty long seconds. The silence was intense.

"I'm sorry too," he told her. "What should I do to help you?"

Jack and Pete met at breakfast. Pete looked fresh, but Jack hadn't slept so well, worrying about the disagreement with Lilia. He had been at his table for fifteen minutes already.

"Did you speak to Lilia?" he asked.

Pete looked across from buttering some toast. "Not yet," he said. "Guess she'll be down soon."

"I called her room this morning, but no answer."

"She'll be here."

Jack drank some coffee and tried to eat, but something wasn't letting him relax. "I'll go to her room and check she's OK, he told Pete. "Be back in a minute."

He took the lift to her floor and followed the passageway to her door. It was open, the maid in tidying up and cleaning.

"Morning," he said to her. "Did you see the lady from this room?"

"No sir," the girl replied. "I am just tidying up. The guest must be away because the bed was made."

An alarm clanged in Jack's head. "The bed was made?" he asked stupidly. The maid confirmed.

He looked around the room, noting clothes still hanging in the wardrobe, a bag on a case-stand. Through the door of the bathroom he could see washing kit. He calmed down a bit. She must have woken-up early and had a walk somewhere. He headed for the breakfast room, told Pete what he'd learned.

"Let's have a look around the hotel," the SAS man suggested. "You know we were all complaining about being penned in here. Maybe she went for an early swim, or even a walk to the park."

"I'll check the pool and the gym, you do the restaurants, lobby and bar. Should be shut, but just in case."

"Meet you in the reception in ten minutes."

"Have you ever fired a gun?" Ahmed asked her.

"Never," she told him, wondering what this young man in front of her must be thinking. Here she was, a Syrian living in the UK, a woman with no experience of fighting, offering to take on the Syrian Army. "But I can learn."

"It's not only about shooting," he said softly. "It's about killing people. People from our own country. Not everyone's cut out to do this."

He spoke quietly and without any real emotion. She wondered how old he was — she thought not more than eighteen — marvelled at the maturity he showed. "I can only try. But I cannot sit back and do nothing anymore. I need to help save my country, or die trying."

"There are other ways to help us," he reasoned with her. "We need money. Money buys arms and then we can resist the Army. Money feeds our people." He stood, putting the AK47 at the back of the room, then returning to his place on the floor. "You can lobby politicians. Not here, but where you are living outside of our country. They can apply pressure and stop the killing. Nothing we do here will stop it. It is beyond us."

"Then why do you fight?"

"Because we can do nothing else. We can be tortured, imprisoned and killed by the regime, as it has been for years, or we can fight back. You can leave, do something that has more effect on Syria and its people. We cannot."

She thought about this. The boy was probably right, but right now she just wanted to get physically involved in the battle, not only mentally. "Maybe you try and do the wrong things."

"You can do better."

It wasn't really phrased as a question: more as a statement of fact. He meant that she was worth more to them fighting outside of Syria, fighting with words, using the media to pressurise politicians, who in turn would put pressure on the Syrian leader. She thought about it, thought again about his age. He was wise beyond his years, but what a horrible way to have to be educated.

"Perhaps you can do better too," she replied.

He smiled at her. "An expert in guerrilla warfare too?"

She returned the smile, acknowledging that she must have sounded a little pompous, entering a war zone and knowing all of the answers. She looked to the door of the hide-out, then back to the boy. "Maybe you are targeting the wrong things."

He breathed deeply, long inhale, slow exhale. "Our leader was a senior figure in the university. He plans what we do, where we hit." It was his turn to look at the stairs climbing out of the room. "He tells us we must wear them down, turn the soldiers from their officers. Divide loyalties. It works. Many have changed to our side already."

"But how long does this process take? How many more must die?"

"I sometimes ask the same question, but I am just a boy."

She reached across, taking a bottle of water from close to Ahmed. "May I?"

He nodded. "It's not from a supermarket, so maybe not the best. But you are welcome to use whatever I have."

She took a short swig, the warm, slightly brown water catching in her throat. She coughed.

"I warned you," he grinned.

She spluttered a little longer, smiled, but then became serious. "I think the only way to stop this is to take Assad out of the game." It was out, it was straightforward, and if heard in the wrong places, it would have her dead in minutes. He wasn't smiling anymore.

"I think the same."

Pete was first at the lobby and talking to the doorman.

"She left here late last night. His friend was on duty, but everyone knows Lilia." He looked anxious. "No-one's sure if she came back yet. She said something about visiting a friend."

Jack's colour faded from his face, his legs felt weak. "Holy shit," he said. "The stupid bitch!"

"Let's keep calm, Jack. Maybe she went to the park to see Jaf. Let's go there." He hurried the older man out of the door and away from the hotel entrance. "Come on mate. We have to keep our heads and think. Now." he said, silently, but with an edge to it.

They were at the edge of the park and Pete moved them towards the boy's den. Jack was moving, but on autopilot. He said nothing.

Pete left him at the edge of the bushes and went in, to where he'd first seen Jaf. Blankets were there, but no boys. It looked like they had left in a hurry — food was still there, clothes, water — but it wasn't damaged, so it didn't appear they were chased out or lost a battle to rivals. Things were tidy, just not organized. He came back out.

"Not there. Looks like they are coming back though."

Jack was sat on the grass, head in hands. "I should have made her talk yesterday. I thought she needed space, but it looks like I got it wrong."

"Not your fault Jack. Remember for her it's personal. Her country, her people, her husband died for this. She was always too caught up in this."

"What do we do?"

Pete thought a minute. "We stay here and wait a while. She knows no-one else."

Pete sat down on the grass next to his friend. His head was also in a spin, but his training was making him think. They had guessed back in UK that Jack and Lilia had become a bit too close: Now he could see that Jack was sick with worry, his mind not functioning.

He had to get Lilia back to get Jack on a level again. The problem was that he needed a functional Jack to help him.

The boys were the only common link they all had, so he settled in to wait.

Chapter Nineteen

25th August 2013, London, UK

"We have to pull them out. With the increased violence right now, how much chance does a group of three have against two armies. Both the rebels and the loyalists are vicious. They will kill anyone they don't trust. We're not talking about them getting caught out and their visas getting revoked."

"I understand your worries Sir, but we have no other plan, and this thing took a good while to set-up," Clive replied to the MP. "I'd let it run for now. They are not inexperienced."

"We have one young SAS lad, an old soldier and a woman with no military background at all. I'd call that inexperienced. Add to that out-gunned!"

The conversation had rolled around and around this theme for about an hour now with no progress. The government was getting nervous — a team of armed UK nationals lifted in Syria would be great for the press.

No-one could argue with the last line from the minister. Out-gunned. Three people against two armies.

"I'll call our man in Lebanon and arrange a tactical withdrawal," Clive announced after a minute. "Give me a couple of days."

The Commanding Officer of 22 SAS Regiment put down the phone. He thought about what he now knew and what he could do.

Peter Davies was a good young officer. He'd been with the Regiment for three years now, seen active service with them and with his cavalry unit before that. He was a great shot, a cool head under stress, and someone good to have at your side in troubled times. He was fit as a lop, a good man for a party when the chance arose, and he had no ties.

But right now he was a little out of his depth.

The Colonel started squiggling on a piece of paper, words, symbols, numbers. He poured a tot of whiskey into a crystal tumbler. His wife was watching a mindless soap, so he busied himself with pulling together some kind of a plan.

His best plans were always assisted by a Bushmills whiskey. He smiled.

Colin was sitting at the bar of his hotel in Beirut enjoying a beer and the scenery, though he could never tell his wife this. The girls here were gorgeous, and the beer more than acceptable. His phone rang. Glancing at the display, he saw it was London.

"Colin Rutherford," the MI6 man chimed. "How can I help?"

On the other end of the line, Clive filled him in on the latest decisions. He explained that nerves had got the better of their political masters, and the team needed to be extracted, quickly and quietly. He was careful in what he said, even though both devices were encoded. In this day and age, you never knew for sure.

"I'll get in touch and come back to you in the morning," Colin told him. "It's eight at night here, so a little late to start anything serious happening, but I'll give them a buzz."

Jack took the call but handed the phone to Pete. They'd been in the park all day except for a short break when Pete had insisted they had some food. That had been about three hours back, and still no sign of the boys.

Listening to the one side of the conversation he could hear, Jack got the gist of it, Pete explaining that Lilia was gone and they had no idea where, that extraction was not possible right now. He reached for the phone. "We can't leave Colin. We leave as a team or not at all."

"I hear you Jack, but I would prefer two of you back than none of you."

"I will stay. Pete can go."

Silence at the other end. Pete could feel Colin's brain churning, even from Beirut.

At last Colin spoke. "I'll tell them I couldn't get you. That the system is reported down. That I will try again in the morning." He paused. "But tomorrow we must have a plan."

The Colonel put down the phone. He googled a page on his laptop, pulled a number for a company mobile phone in Syria. Called it. Got a mouthful of Arabic and cut the connection.

They weren't answering. That either meant they couldn't answer, or they didn't wish to answer.

He scrolled through some numbers on his secure line. Pressed one and heard the call answered almost immediately. "Hi Smithy, the Boss here. Prepare the teams on 'strip duty' for immediate dispatch to Lebanon in the morning. Move order will be finalised by ten o'clock Zulu."

Peter Davies would get his back-up.

She fired a weapon for the first time: an AK, the same as many rebels worldwide broke their teeth on.

"Relax with it," Ahmed told her.

It was ten o'clock at night and they were in a deserted area about a mile from his den. His people had checked for government forces and found none, but they knew that the firing would attract attention, so time was of the essence.

The gun was at her shoulder, the safety on single shot. She was surprised at the harshness of the kick and the deafening sound. She released her fifth shot and actually hit the oil drum about fifty yards ahead.

"You want to try a burst?" He moved close to her, moving the weapon from her shoulder to waist level. "Doesn't matter if you get a hit. A burst will keep heads down. It's scary to be on the wrong end of bullets."

She flicked the change lever to burst as he had shown her that day in training. Held the weapon as Ahmed had directed her. Pulled the trigger and was shocked by the violent movement in the AK47. It was as if it had a life of its own.

"STOP!" Ahmed yelled.

She released the trigger, pushed the lever to safe.

"Short bursts," he told her, shouting into her ear. "Otherwise no control."

She went through the drill to unload the gun. Her ears pinged, hearing as shot as the weapon.

"Back to our hole," Ahmed told her. "Now we should talk."

Pete slept in the grass as easily as he did in a four-poster bed. His training meant the sleep was light, but it was an art form he had perfected during his years of military service. He could sleep anywhere, at any hour of the day, whenever the schedule allowed it.

It wasn't the same for Jack. He tried. He paced. He checked the bushes himself. He worried.

It was around midnight and Pete suddenly sat-up, head tilted to one side, ear pointing to where he thought he heard the sound. Jack looked at him, prowling back and forth again. "Shhh!" Pete directed. He opened his mouth slightly and Jack looked hard in to the blackness in the direction the younger man indicated. Nothing.

"Get down. Someone's coming."

Jack dropped into the grass, the senior man, but knowing that Pete had a technical edge over him when it came to combat experience.

Minutes later, body forms emerged out of the gloom. The boys had returned.

Pete's hand rested on Jack's shoulder, requesting him to stay down. A sudden move and a loose bullet could destroy a million years of military training in one second. They watched the boys come forward towards their hide-out, calm but careful. They reached their home in the bush and started laying out bedding. Some lay down and slept with only a jacket over them. They were tired out.

When everything was relaxed, Pete crawled forward.

"Hello Jaf," he announced the only name he knew. "We are friends. We need to talk to you."

The walk back to the underground shelter was slow and careful. Lilia's ears were still ringing from firing the Kalashnikov, but she somehow also felt exhilarated from the experience. She was finally doing something for Syria.

As they made the final approach, one of Ahmed's troops signalled a halt. They all went into a crouched position. Ahmed moved silently forward. Words were exchanged. He edged round a small wall, looking ahead. The man was right. Troops were around his home, one coming out of the hole in the rubble. An APC stood close by, a gunner behind its heavy machine gun. The home was lost.

He came back to his people and led them in the opposite direction. They needed a new place to stay.

They holed up in a temporary hide-out, the front, by the roadside, fully collapsed. They managed to find access at the rear, a room with two exits, both away from the street. From a still standing upstairs window in the house next door, they had a view onto what remained of the street. A sentry would be there all night, an advance warning of danger.

Lilia was tired, but still excited from the firing of the machine gun. Ahmed was checking everybody was fed and watered, that a shift pattern was agreed for the night.

He returned to the room.

"You are crazy," he told Lilia. "But you are brave. I am proud you are a Syrian."

Lilia blushed, unsure how to respond to such a compliment from a young man.

"But so are you," she eventually told him.

Sitting on the bare floor facing each other, she started to tell him about her life. Her start in Syria, meeting a British soldier, falling in love and marrying the man, and his murder here in the country she loved, by the people he was still fighting now. At times tears rolled down her cheeks, but she kept the tale going.

"And now I am here," she completed. "I have to do something to help." She looked up, noticing for the first time that Ahmed also had tears on his cheeks.

"I really don't want you here," he eventually said.

"But it's my country too…" she started.

"Please," he interrupted. "Let me finish my words."

He wiped his cheek with the back of a dirty hand, smearing dust over his face. "My men shouldn't see me this way," he said smiling.

She smiled sadly back at him. "They can't," she told him. "They're all asleep."

"I don't want you here because I don't want to be responsible for the death of three women I like," he told her. She looked directly at him, her face reddening slightly.

"Let me tell you my tale…"

It was gone two o'clock in the morning when the two stopped talking. Following Ahmed's story, they had discussed the mess that was now Damascus: how the rebels lived; people who remained; food shortages; power outages; deaths of friends and loved ones. Everyone had lost someone. They also reflected on the good times before the troubles.

Ahmed walked through to the sentry in the next house, saying he must check the security. He really needed time to think, time alone. He already found himself deeply connected to Lilia, someone who understood his hurt and who had experienced her own. She was somehow like his mother, possibly due to the age difference, but also reminded him of Saumaya. She had been a very determined girl, and Lilia was the same. Peas in a pod.

He wished that he could persuade her to leave, but at the same time wanted her to stay around. She was a kindred soul.

He checked the sentry and returned to the hide out. Lilia already slept.

Lilia lay on a dirty, dusty carpet that covered the hard concrete that was her bed. She had a jacket under her head to make things better, but it was anything but comfortable. In the next room she could hear a man snoring. Her mind was racing from the discussions with Ahmed: how could one so young have so much experience of life?

She was shocked at the stories she had heard. The rebels were hunted like animals by the army, but they still had eat, drink and sleep; they needed weapons and ammunition to keep the battle going, often stealing it from the military. She had learned that they were organised and coordinated — not as a battalion or regiment would be set up, but still with a central planning and organisation — this setting the tasks that the groups, or cells, had to complete. Sometimes the cells operated individually, and at other times they joined up and formed larger forces.

She had connected with Ahmed at some simple, basic level: they both loved their country and they both had loved and lost people very dear to them.

She thought about the tears from the boy's eyes when he described the rape and murder of his mother and girlfriend, when he spoke of the love for his father who had also been taken. These events were where he found the passion to do what he did now.

Helping him was not an option, it was something she needed to do. She also had a score to settle.

Chapter Twenty

26th August 2013, Damascus, Syria

Jack woke up at seven in the morning, five hours after he'd gone to bed in the hotel. He'd been all up for going off into the city to find Lilia, but the boys were exhausted and as Pete had rightly said, they were not prepared at all. In the end he had relented and gone to his bed.

He showered and dressed quickly, anxious to get out of the hotel.

They had weapons in the car. It looked like they would need them sooner than expected.

Pete had been up an hour, already a plan formed in his head. He sat in the lobby area, close to the restaurant entrance, watching people taking an early breakfast. He had a three-day-old English newspaper on his lap, something one of the UN people or a reporter had brought when they'd arrived. He'd read it the day before but pretended to read it again.

His attention changed suddenly. He had seen what he wanted. Two pressmen headed for the restaurant, discussing whether or not they would finally be allowed to visit Ghouta that day, and if so, what would they find. Pete put down the paper and followed them in, standing behind them as they gave their room numbers to a waitress before being seated.

He had heard what he wanted. Pretending to have forgotten his wallet, he patted his rear trouser pocket. "Be back in a minute," he told the girl.

He took the lift to the third floor, looking for the room number he'd overheard. Three-one-five. The corridor was deserted.

Pulling out a set of lock-picks he made short work of the hotel security, opened the door and went inside. In the corner on the chair, were the man's clothes from the night before. On top of them was a press pass attached to a CNN neck-lanyard.

The man in the picture looked surprisingly similar to Jack.

He left the room.

Jack was at breakfast wondering where Pete was. He was anxious to go to the boys and find Lilia. He forced himself to eat, as he knew it might be the last food for the day, but the eating was mechanical, not enjoyable.

Pete entered, looking for his table. Eye contact made, moving towards him.

"Morning. How are you?" Pete's eyes were digging behind the face, trying to see how stable his colleague was.

"Fine. Just want to get on with things. From what the boys said we have quite a walk."

"We're driving." This was a surprise.

"But troops are everywhere. We wouldn't last five minutes out there."

"Oh yes we will Mister Ricardo." Pete held the pass under the table so Jack could see it. "And I'm your camera man."

He grinned.

They had moved to the third floor of a bombed out building, the room complete with four walls, floor and ceiling, but the glass from the windows was long gone. Wallpaper peeled off the walls, which was possibly a good thing, as the previous occupier clearly had no taste. Mattresses had been fashioned into seating areas. A small gas cooker was in one corner, a pan on it filled with tepid water from when coffee had been brewed earlier.

Ahmed slept.

Lilia stood, looking out of the glassless window and wondered if she had made the right decision to run. She would have given anything for a shower, but running water was not an option. She was tired, had slept awhile, but now couldn't relax and rest. She could see one of Ahmed's men moving around outside, ensuring their safety.

What would Jack be thinking? She knew in her heart that he would be beside himself with worry and hoped he would try nothing stupid. Young Pete would be a leveller — his training made him a safe bet to stabilise things back at the hotel.

She heard a helicopter somewhere overhead and looked to see that the sentry had disappeared. It was a crazy situation when school teachers, mechanics, shop workers and cleaners had been forced to become killers. It was also amazing how swiftly they had become militarised, knowing when to fight and when to hide.

The helicopter moved into her field of view and she slipped to the edge of the window, keeping out of sight. She knew police helicopters in the UK sometimes had heat seeking equipment fitted and wondered if this aircraft had something fitted to pick up her heat-signature. She wondered about the sentry down there, and if he knew about such things.

The throb of the rotors moved closer, then passed and faded.

She wondered what her former husband would have thought about her move back to the city. Also if he would have approved of her liaison with Jack. She thought he would.

Sitting down on a mattress, she tried to sleep again. Ahmed had explained to her that most things happened at night when the Assad forces had less control. It meant they had a lot of time to kill.

Jaf was in the back seat of the Rover, probably the first time he had been in a car, or at least the first time he remembered it. The boys had agreed he should go; he was the youngest and the troops were normally sorry for him. It might be an advantage.

The cover story was that Jack was a reporter, Pete the cameraman, and their budget was limited. Jaf was young and cheap but knew the city.

The problem for Jaf was that he only knew the routes on foot. That meant he could take alleys, shortcuts through buildings, footbridges. In the vehicle everything came at him much faster, and he had to stick to useable roads. It wasn't easy for the young boy.

They passed their first military roadblock. The ID pass had been waved through after only a cursory glance, the camera equipment intentionally on display on the back seat. A cinch.

They took a right turn at the direction of the boy, but soon realised it was a street going nowhere.

A foot patrol dismounted from an APC over to their right, the men in full disruptive pattern camouflage and webbing jackets, weapons held ready. Their commander formed them up and began walking them towards a building, alert for snipers. The APC gunner moved the barrel of the machine gun over the building, watching for danger. No-one seemed too interested in the white Range Rover doing a three-point-turn to their rear.

Jack and Pete watched the troops. "They are pretty well drilled," Jack commented. "You can see they know their job, no screaming and shouting."

"Pretty well armed too," Pete added.

Jaf was silent. He couldn't understand why they would say good things about his enemy.

Colin rang the number. Heard the electronic ringing at the other end. Waited.

No-one picked-up.

"Shit!" he mouthed to himself.

It was seven in the morning, five in the UK. He still had a couple of hours before his lords and master's started asking questions.

He headed for breakfast.

Jaf was sure he was at the right place. Of course there were no street signs, no number on the door or anything like that, but the area looked right, felt right. He got out of the car and looked for signs of Ahmed or his troops.

The British soldiers also got out of the vehicle, looking around for danger.

"Is this the place?" the older man asked.

The boy looked around again for landmarks. "It is, but nobody seems to be here. Normally someone would have stopped me by now."

"Could it be the wrong street?"

Pausing and giving another all-round scan, the boy shook his head. "It is here." He started walking towards a pile of rubble that had once been a house. The soldiers followed, confused. Both were further puzzled when the boy climbed the heap and then disappeared. "Come on," they heard him call.

At the top of the pile they looked down to see him and understood. The room was maybe ten feet long and wide, the roof formed by the old cellar ceiling and the rubble. They could see it had been abandoned rather than vacated: personal items were still there, old clothes and cooking utensils, a picture of a woman and a girl, the woman not so old and the girl only a teenager.

"They've gone," Jaf said. "Soldiers must have found the place."

Jack felt a ripple of panic run through him, starting in the stomach. "Captured?" he asked.

"Don't think so," the boy was looking around, pacing the corners and dark patches. "No blood. Couldn't have been shot or beaten."

Jack looked at Pete who nodded. "So where are they?"

"I guess they had to move."

"So how do we find them?"

A shrug of the shoulders. "We look around. Ask questions," he answered as if everyone knew this. "Let's go."

They'd driven around for about three hours in the wrecked neighbourhood. Jaf thought they could not have gone too far: they were walking, he reasoned.

They turned into another broken street to be confronted by an army roadblock. Jack pulled the Rover slowly up to the checkpoint, window rolling down for a corporal with a hand out. "Hi," he smiled, masking the nervousness he felt. "OK to have a look around?"

The corporal looked into the car, noting the occupants and seeing no obvious threat.

"English?" he asked.

Jack took the CNN ID tag and held it towards him. "I am but working for these guys. Trying to get a story for the news."

The man looked from the ID to the face, but not too carefully. He seemed satisfied. "And him?" he said, pointing to Pete.

"My cameraman." He pointed to the television equipment in the back by Jaf.

"What about the boy?"

"Our local guide. Said he knew his way around and would help us. Cost twenty dollars."

The soldier scowled, not looking impressed. "Where do you go to? This is not a safe area." He gesticulated at the shells of buildings. "Not safe."

"We don't go inside," said Pete smiling. "Could we make a film of you and your men?"

"Film? With me?" The corporal was impressed.

"Sure," Jack said, opening his door. "Is it OK?"

"For on television? Big time?"

Pete was playing with the camera on the far side of the car, trying to remember how it worked. He managed to get it switched on and came around the vehicle, pointing the lens at the soldier.

"Why not you get back in the car, and the Major here checks your details?" Pete suggested.

"Yeah, good idea," Jack said. "We can voice-over later in the studio."

For the next five minutes they made three takes of the soldier — the Major according to Pete — checking Jack. The corporal had a quick look at the finished product — about twenty seconds footage – and nodded his head.

"OK. You go now."

With the light fading, they pointed the Rover back towards the hotel. Jaf had spoken to a few people, but no-one seems to know where Ahmed had moved to, or at least if they knew, they weren't willing to share it.

"We try again in the morning," Pete said. "Hard to find anything in the dark, and there's also a bigger chance of us getting caught up in a fire-fight."

They dropped Jaf at the park and cleaned up for dinner.

The fading light signalled the end of the day for some, but the beginning of things for others.

The team led by Ahmed started drifting into the new base around six in the evening. They did not know what the night would bring and wouldn't until Ahmed returned from his meeting with the university lecturer. That would be soon though.

Some nights nothing would happen. Others they would work alone as a group, firing on military patrols from abandoned buildings, setting fire to cars or buildings to cause distractions for other teams, maybe just watching a position and recording how often it was visited by the enemy. Other times they would be coordinated into a larger operation: the attack on Mount Quasioun had been a good and successful example of this.

Lilia watched the men prepare, very aware that she was the only female there. These were men with few laws governing them, and things could turn bad very quickly. She had her hair up under a baseball cap, and wore a shapeless coat, but anyone looking hard enough could not mistake her for what she was, and that was a beautiful woman.

Ahmed returned and gathered his people around him. The night's briefing began.

Chapter Twenty-One

26th August 2013, Hereford, UK

"One of our own is presently enjoying the backstreets and byways of sunny Damascus, and the powers that be have decided it may not be too safe there. Not certain how they deduced that little gem, but that is how it is."

The Colonel addressed the group of twenty officers and men of the Special Air Service in the training theatre.

"A little background: someone in government decided that they would assemble a think-tank to brainstorm what could be done to stop the troubles in Syria. I was asked for an officer to be part of the team and sent Pete Davies. Also on the team was a Major who had spent recent time in Lebanon, so had a feeling for the region; a man from MI6 Middle East desk; and a girl originally from Syria who lives in the UK now."

The gathering in front of him remained silent, though one or two of them had exchanged glances when they were told which of their colleagues was in at the deep end.

"The sessions in London came to the conclusion that the only way to stop the madness that is happening in Syria, was to remove its head. Bashir Al-Assad, in other words." He stood up from the seat he had been in and paced to his left, raising his right arm to make the next point. "Next question was how to do it. Our little team decided perhaps they could do it themselves, and volunteered to go in, to Damascus. Then things got a little out of control." He came back to centre stage and stood behind the chair, hands gripping the back and leaning slightly forward.

"We have all read the reports about the chemical attack at Ghouta, both the newspaper version and what our intelligence have since put together. That attack has sparked an escalation in violence in the city." He paused, thinking about his next phrase.

"Our intrepid decision-makers that sent the team in there, have now decided it would be better if someone got them out." He sat down in the seat.

"So where do you all fit in to this little tale, I can see you wondering?" He smiled. "Good news is you are not going storming into Syria on an Apache helicopter or any other vehicle for that matter. We are contacting our people there and asking them to withdraw, and hopefully they will sneak back out the same way as they sneaked in.

"I just want to put you up on the border in case things don't go as smoothly as we hope. A few of you know Pete, and he's a great soldier, but he's a bit out on a limb right now. I want back-up on hand in case he needs it."

The Admin Sergeant-Major joined him on the stage.

"I want to get us out of here tomorrow morning and be set up on the border tomorrow evening. That means we have quite a lot to do, so I'll hand-over now to Chippy here." He gestured to the SNCO. "He's much better than me at the fine details."

"Thanks Boss," Chippy said. "So guys, we are all pretty much packed I guess, but we will need some equipment to suit the ground we'll be on. I'll break you up in to four groups, and each of you will have a task."

The Colonel left the meeting. He had decided he would also have a flight to Beirut.

The soldiers boarded the two Hercules C130 aircraft at Brize Norton at nine o'clock the following morning. Each aircraft took ten men and two open-top Land Rovers that were secured to the floor of the planes by the RAF Loadmasters.

The SAS men loaded their Bergens, weapons and a cardboard box, containing food for each man, for the journey.

A RAF Flight Lieutenant stepped out of the cockpit and stood on a pile of palletised baggage.

"Morning," he greeted the men in the first C130. "I will be your captain for today's flight, and my loadmaster over there will be your chief purser and stewardess." The soldiers grinned, a couple of wolf-whistles were directed to the moustached RAF man. "We'll be in the air in about six to six-and-a-half hours, depending on the wind up there, and we'll get there in a single hop. Remember these old beasts have been flying since 1954, so if anybody sees any bits falling off, please let me know."

"Bloody Brylcreem Boys," said one of the soldiers. "Don't know they're born."

The pilot headed back in to the cockpit and shortly afterwards the first of four Allison T56-A-15 turboprop engines roared into life.

The SAS men made themselves comfortable on the webbed seats, some of them climbing into the strapped down Land Rovers and trying to sleep.

Not much they could do for the next few hours.

Chapter Twenty-Two

29th August 2013, Damascus, Syria

It was her third night out with the men. The previous two had been largely uneventful — one laid up for an ambush that never happened, and one watching a police station and clocking patrol timings. She hadn't fired a shot in anger yet, hadn't aimed a live round at another fellow human being. She still wondered if she could do this.

The task this evening was, again, an ambush position, occupying a fourth floor of a badly damaged block of flats about two miles from their lay-up point. Intelligence reports had predicted that the enemy patrolled that area on foot. The intention was to wait for a patrol to enter the 'kill-zone', hit two or three of them, then escape to safety out of the rear of the building while the government troops were still reeling from the hit.

Lilia was two windows along from where Ahmed slept on the floor. Every second fighter was resting, and the watchers would change for the off-duty job every two hours. This way no-one was too tired if things didn't happen all night.

She was more accepted now, but still very aware of the interest in her from the fighters, especially the older ones. She didn't panic, but she did worry.

An older man in the next room started snoring, and a rebel went through and kicked his foot. Advertising their position was not a great idea.

She had had a lot of time to think in the last days. Too much time, some would say. She thought about Jack, her hotel bed, clean clothes and a shower. She had brought only a small bag, containing clean underwear and a couple of blouses, with her but, when you lived in the same rooms as men and had no locking doors, when did you change? And with no running water, when did you wash to make the change worthwhile?

She also had time to reflect on the young words of Ahmed. Would one extra gun change the outcome of this conflict? Could she do more demonstrating and lobbying back in London? One gun in a city of guns was hardly a life changer.

Could she get out of it now though? Would the rebels let her walk away, and if she did, how did she return to the hotel?

Her mind was busy as she waited for her first moment of action.

Jack was tired. He had slept badly every night since Lilia had disappeared. Hadn't felt up to eating.

Pete and Jaf had joined him each day searching the streets, talking to locals and soldiers alike, trying to find her. He was certain she was either captured, dead or held hostage by now. A woman living alone in the streets would find it almost impossible he'd decided.

He turned in his bed, trying to find a position where he could find sleep and forget the horrors out there.

Sleep didn't come.

Colin was worried sick. The idiots he loosely called colleagues had left the cell phone off for two days now. Initially he had covered for them with excuse after excuse, but with the SAS team's arrival, this was no longer possible. London had gone ballistic. The Colonel had been more balanced.

"Pete's been with us a good while. If he needed help, he'd ask. If things were bad, he'd be out by now."

"And if he can't get out?" had been the question from London, via the MI6 man. "What if they're caught?"

"I think we may have heard about that by now," the Boss had told him. "Our Mister Assad isn't too shy to tell tales that favour him."

The reassurances hadn't done much to relax him.

No contact was just that: no contact.

Still fighting the internal demons, Lilia had missed the first movement outside the window. When she did note it, her mind rejected it, knowing that this was the moment when the hardest decision was to be made: if she alerted the rest of them, could she kill the man down there?

In the end someone else made the choice for her, a whisper coming from her left. The fighters were waking, alert immediately, as though they had never slept.

The first man from the patrol had come into view from the left of their position, walking carefully, eyes everywhere and gun following. He was nervous because he was the lead soldier, not because it was his first action. As the lead he was exposed first, had no other eyes and ears to assist him, no firepower covering him except to his rear. He was the battering ram into the unknown, and because of this his nerves jangled, his senses were on fire.

A second man came into view, his main focus the opposite side of the street, but swinging his gaze often in an all-around motion.

Then a third, attention on their block of flats.

They had appeared in the rebels' field-of-vision from the left and, before the buildings blocked them from view again, they would need to cover about three hundred and fifty feet of open and exposed roadway. That left the men in the building plenty of time to get organised and agree their targets. Ahmed held up an open hand, signalling them to hold their fire.

A fourth man had appeared, then a fifth. More and they would be outnumbered, but that wasn't important: the plan was to kill and run, not to exterminate the whole enemy.

The first man was in the centre of the open ground — the killing zone — a spacing of around thirty feet between the brothers-in-arms. They were well trained, maintaining the patrol distance, not getting nervy and closing up the space.

It was time.

Ahmed dropped his arm and all hell broke loose for the soldiers below them.

The first man found cover behind a burnt out car, trying to burrow his way into the concrete for cover. He was lucky.

Number two and three weren't so. They were taken in the first burst of bullets, two catching it in the chest and abdomen, and the third with a head-shot. Both were dead in seconds.

The fourth man ran away — the fight or flight instinct kicking in — and made it to the rubble on the far side of the clearing. He was lucky, bullets ricocheting around him, but nothing coming close. He pissed himself anyway, unable to believe he was alive.

The sixth man appeared as the rounds went down, and he and number five took hits, five dead and number six catching two rounds in the thigh. He lay on the edge of the kill zone screaming his heart out but managed to haul his damaged body clear of another bullet and into cover.

The other five men in the patrol found cover and returned fire.

Ahmed had seen enough. Blasting a whistle, he turned towards the rear of the building, looking left and right to see his team had taken notice. Sometimes a man needed pulling away from the action, hooked on the adrenalin and power the weapon had given him.

They all followed.

He dashed through the door at the rear of the room. Something was wrong.

Lights splashed around the dark interior of the flat. He reached a rear window, and the reason behind the lights was explained.

Three APCs discharged Assad troops at the rear of the building. He directed a man to the front, only to be told the same was happening there. He'd been caught out. The ambusher had been ambushed. Troops front and rear.

In a straight firefight he knew he had no chance. There were probably thirty enemy on either side of the building, and he had only five men — wrong, four and a women.

"Every man for himself!" he yelled, and they all moved in their own chosen directions.

Ahmed headed up the stairwell, already hearing soldiers at the base of the building, clearing rooms and coming steadily upwards. There was no way down, and he hadn't checked the access to adjoining buildings. Up was the only hope. Breathlessly, he continued the climb.

The final door to the roof was locked, but only as a fire exit would be locked and he kicked the bar on it, smashing it back on its hinges. He was out. He went to the side of the building, assessing his chances. No way off the roof.

He looked around him, air-conditioning units everywhere, but not really providing any real or lasting cover.

Water header tanks…

Lilia hid. She hadn't even fired a shot, the chaos of the ambush had stunned her. The follow-up terrified her and she had no plan for what to do now.

She found a small storage room — like a walk-in wardrobe in an up-market flat — in what had no doubt once been the bedroom of the flat. It had once been used to store clean towels, bed linen, shoes and clothes she guessed, but was now just a tip for water bottles and food containers. She entered it and tried to hide.

She had always thought that her husband's death had been the worst day of her life.

It had just been surpassed.

She was terrified. The smell of sweat, fear and bodies, the sound of the injured and the boots of soldiers powering up staircase, filled her senses. Even the stench from the weapons smelt different to the time spent practising with them.

She burrowed under the rubbish.

There were a number of water tanks on the roof, some were clear plastic so out of the question. He climbed on top of a red one, but the inspection hole was too small. The next one he clambered up had no inspection port at all, and his spirit fell through his shoes. The noise from below was getting louder. Shots were fired, screams echoed up to the roof. No way out.

He climbed on top of the next tank, his Kalashnikov whacking him in the back of the head as it moved loose on its sling.

Thank you God, Allah, anyone.

An inspection lid the size of a manhole cover. He twisted it, stiff at first, but coming free. Lifting it he could smell that the water had stood for some time, a sewer-like quality to it, stinging his nostrils. A thin, greenish layer of algae floated on the water, staining his clothes as he lowered himself through the hatch and into the muck. He eased himself in, trying to keep the weapon dry, even though old fighters had told him it would fire full of sand and underwater. No point testing the theory.

The voices of the government troops grew louder.

He lowered the lid behind him and managed half a turn.

"They were here!" cried the first soldier, showing his NCO the fresh shell cases and the food and drink that had been deserted.

"Three are dead," the Corporal replied, knowing they had taken three men down on the stairs.

"Maybe that was all of them?"

"Could be. We search the place anyway. Kill all of the rats that we find."

The rooms were bare, but they kept looking.

The soldier entered the small box-room.

She felt they must smell her fear, hear her heart pounding. The small room and the rubbish seemed to amplify the sounds.

Footsteps, getting closer. Very close.

Something was amiss. He was about to leave the small rubbish-filled space, but something was bugging him.

It was just wrong. He looked out of the room, then back into it, trying to make his mind see what the inconsistency was. Then it dawned. The rubbish was all piled in one corner, in a heap, not spread around. Could have been luck, could have been…

His rifle pointing to the pile of bottles, papers, clothes and junk, he lifted his right boot and kicked some of it away. Kicked a little more, still not sure.

A foot appeared.

"OUT!" he yelled. "OUT OR I SHOOT!"

A body rolled clear of the debris, jeans, a baggy jacket and a baseball hat. Again, his mind said something was not right… He grabbed the person, pulling the hat away from the head. "A woman," he shouted, sounding like he'd just won the jackpot of a major lottery. "I have found a woman!"

He slammed Lilia against the wall, grabbing a handful of the jacket at the same time, the zipper breaking open. The air burst from her lungs as she hit the wall, stunned. He caught the pullover underneath with both hands, turning her towards a second wall, tearing it, and with it the top two blouse buttons popped off. Her grubby five-day-old brassiere came into view, her chest heaving from fear and shock.

"I'm right. A woman."

Another soldier came to the doorway and Lilia began to gather her senses, swinging a boot at the first man. They grabbed her, forced her out of the small room and against a wall in the bedroom. A third man joined, holding her as the first soldier pushed his hand inside of the blouse.

"Now we can have some fun," said number two, undoing his jacket with one hand. "Sex with a rebel whore."

Lilia was exhausted from trying to fight three men and could see where this was going. Rape was the only possible outcome.

"STOP! ENOUGH!" a voice rang out. "GET AWAY FROM HER."

She was released and fell to the floor. An officer stood close by. He looked at the men.

"We are soldiers, not rapists. Take her to the APC. We need to interrogate her. Find out who are the leaders."

Three hours later Ahmed climbed out of the stinking water. He had heard them from his hide-out on the roof. Searching and laughing. They had found the girl, one of them had said that. The animal had said he was going to have sex with her at the first opportunity, as soon as the officers and intelligence people had got any information out of the bitch, done their official duty. He had said that she was going to enjoy meeting a man with a large weapon, not an untrained terrorist.

Ahmed was careful: they may have left someone behind, maybe a secondary ambush to the one that had already killed his people.

There was nothing. They had gone.

He was still a boy. He had lost his men. He had lost a woman who looked similar to his girl. Nothing was right, it was as bad as he could remember since that dark day the soldiers came to his house.

Lilia had become something personal — not Saumaya, not his mother, but a third women who had been ripped from his protection by the Assad military. He was a failure, a boy who was trying to be something more than he really was. How many more must he lose?

He sat on the roof and cried.

Chapter Twenty-Three

1st September 2013, Damascus, Syria

She'd been in the cell two days, or that's what she thought. Could have been longer, with no light entering the small box. She slept when she could, had nightmares about what had happened and what could come next. Saw no way out of hell.

The first night they had secured her hands with plastic wraps used for electrical cables, stuffed her in the back of the armoured car, closed the doors. Maybe half an hour later they had completed the search of the building and the soldiers had climbed in with her. The vehicle hammered its way over the rubble, and then the tyres had sounded a mid-pitched growl as they hummed on the paved roads.

No-one had spoken to her, but eyes undressed her. Her jacket still hung a little open, and with no hands she couldn't repair the damage done to the jumper and blouse. They looked at her breasts in the off-white bra and imagined. She could see the thoughts in their faces.

She knew that she was in deep trouble, and knew that perhaps this was even too much of an optimistic assessment for the plight she now found herself in.

In the morning a man had come in to the cell. Maybe thirty, not shaved for a day or two, grey-black stubble around a square jaw, his grey slacks and a white shirt, greyer around the collar. He'd been reasonable, asking what she'd been doing in the building, who she was with, where they came from, how the rebel cell was structured and so on. She lied but soon came unstuck when he mentioned the AK47 they'd found her with. She lied again, saying the rebels had found her there and forced her to join them. He didn't believe her and stormed out.

She'd been left alone. Contemplating her lies. Maybe they were checking the stories. Maybe it was a psychological thing.

The next day — if it was day — two men had come in while she slept. She woke-up to a boot in the stomach, making her spasm as she tried to vomit, but with almost no food in her, just dry heaving. Another boot caught her in the ribcage, another under the jaw. From the bliss of sleep to the agony of real life. She was certain her ribs were broken, sure this was the end. You can only accept so much pain, and then your body and mind will shut down. It's a protection mechanism. Now she really thought she was going to die, and part of her mind thought this may be better than being raped to death. At least she retained a little pride this way.

The boots kept coming in, and consciousness deserted her.

She woke up, pain everywhere and the taste of blood in her mouth. There was a jagged edge to one of her front teeth when her tongue caught on it, and she realised at least one of her teeth was broken, the nerves exposed to the cool cell air. A sharp pain. She spat out a piece of the enamel, her tongue visiting other damaged areas of her mouth and lips.

She tried to get up, staggered, but the energy was totally gone. Her ribs hurt like hell, the underside of her jaw agony.

She lay back down and slept on the floor that was covered in her own blood.

Ahmed remembered that the girl had been brought to him by the boy, and that the boy had mentioned other Westerners, men, possibly military. Something about the Four Seasons Hotel next to a park.

What type of military? He pondered. Only one type here in Damascus, and they belonged to Assad. Was she a spy? He was certain this could not be so, but there again, why not? Sent to infiltrate the rebels and pull them down. Why not? Times were hard, so why not employ a woman to do what the men had failed to do? That perhaps she was out to get them?

Something in his soul told him this was not possible. In the short time they had spent together, a bond had formed. She was like him, he knew she too had suffered a massive loss.

That left only one place to go.

He went, found the boy and was led to the men.

With the second beating her pride left her. She soiled her pants, wet herself, begging for the kicks and punches to stop. Her damaged ribs were rubbing against internal organs, the flesh screaming with pain. She wished for oblivion, prayed to pass out, anything to escape. A red-white haze blocked her vision. Her teeth hurt with every single breath, even though her ribs hurt more. And having your ribs booted meant you had no choice but to swallow air. If they had said to her, OK, let's have sex, she would have grabbed them both. Anything to escape the agony her body felt. It wasn't fair.

She knew that she would die here, it was only a matter of how long it would take.

The men stopped, breathing hard, tired and sweaty from the brutal beating they had just handed-out.

"We'll be back tomorrow," one of them wheezed. "If you don't answer what we ask, then it's the same again. If that doesn't work then the bastards who found you can have you."

She knew what the soldiers would do. That was the end. Perhaps it was a blessing.

Pete had needed to slow Jack down, stopped him going straight to the Rover and tearing down town. He knew that the army were not likely to admit to holding the Lilia, and certainly wouldn't just be handing her over to them. Right now maybe they didn't know why she was here, didn't know about the team, and a couple of Brits storming in and demanding her release would probably only lead to them giving her an additional interrogation. And he knew from his colleagues who'd been captured in Iraq just what that could entail. Nails pulled, teeth yanked out, fingers chopped off…

He shivered at the thought. How could human beings even think to do such things?

He had sent Jack to check the weapons in the car, give them a clean and oil and have the magazines stripped, cleaned and then loaded. It allowed him to be alone. Allowed him to use the secure phone and talk to Colin. His news was bad, but Colin's was at least giving him a shred of hope.

"A team from Hereford?" he checked he'd heard right. "That's brilliant."

Colin slowed him down. "They don't want them entering Syria if possible but thought maybe they could assist at the border or something. Your Colonel says he'll go in if he deems it necessary though. Seems that guy will do anything for you guys."

Pete could imagine the Boss ignoring the rules. You didn't get to his position in Special Forces by just following rules.

"We have been told where they might be holding her," he informed his colleague. "We'll go down there in daylight to recce it. Maybe we can do something."

"London want you out Pete. Quickly. There's talk of airstrikes after the Sarin attack, and we don't need any friendly-fire incidents."

"If we get her, we'll need out fast. I don't think she'll be in a great condition."

Colin was silent for a minute, his imagination running scenarios for Lilia. They weren't nice images.

"Call me before you do anything."

The main detention centre that the army was utilising was located outside the city next to Damascus International Airport. This is where Ahmed had heard they would have the girl, the place where he fully expected her to be, cowering in a corner of a cell with some bastard of a government soldier beating her to a pulp.

They drove out there in the Rover, Ahmed in the front with Pete, Jack and the kid in the back. The press pass had got them through one military checkpoint, but no-one was confident it could last much longer, certain that the loss would, by now, be reported. It was how far to push it: Jack was all for storming in there right now, while Pete thought that maybe parking up and walking in was better, cameras and all. He wanted a reconnaissance. As usual, in the end, it was a compromise.

They parked in the main airport parking area. Pete was surprised that the ticket machines still functioned: deep into a war and people were still trying to make money.

Jack was at least still thinking, realising that all of them walking in would attract attention, so he split them into two groups: Ahmed and Jaf would stroll around and see what they could learn from locals; he and Pete to carry on being journalists, cameras and mics in hand. They headed towards the main airport buildings, stopping occasionally to sight the camera on parked aircraft, as if they were making a story for the outside world.

Coming around a corner to the main administrative building they found themselves confronted by two armed soldiers guarding the entrance door. Pete raised the camera, pointing it towards them, but the soldiers raised their weapons, pointing and waving at them, clearly not wanting to be filmed. Jack held his hands in front of him, one with the microphone, the other open and in a gesture of apology.

"Sorry, sorry," he told them. "We were just making a movie report for CNN and thought we could show you in it."

The senior soldier — who also spoke the best English — moved towards them. "No movie in this area," he said. "No civilian here. Go away."

"What is so secret here?" Pete asked from behind Jack. He was a little nervous as the rifles were still pointed their way.

"Go! Now! Only soldiers here."

Saying their sorries, they turned and headed back around the corner.

"Let's try the other side of the building," Pete suggested. "They obviously don't want people like us around here."

"That could mean we are in the right place," Jack surmised.

They tracked along the building's wall and turned at the far end to see the side opposite the guarded doorway. The scene was the same, with two guards at the main door. They went through the same act with the same results, this time with the guards threatening to confiscate the camera.

"Get out of this area," they were told. "Or we put you in a cell for a night or two."

They walked back towards the car, checking for other buildings with guards, but finding none. It looked like they had found their target.

Ahmed and Jaf were already in the car park, but sensibly not hovering around beside the car.

"I spoke to a few locals, low level people. They tell me the holding cells are in the building over there." He pointed towards the building where the two soldiers from UK had been. "One of them is a cleaner for the offices there. She told me that many rebel fighters and suspects are held there, some in a dreadful state. One of them is a woman."

"Who was the commander of your fighting group?" the man with a scar down one side of his jaw bawled. It looked like an old shrapnel wound, and his face was badly disfigured by it. He tried to hide it with a thin black beard, but in the area of the scar no hair grew. "It's time now for answers, or things are going to get much worse for you."

"I have told you, I wasn't with them. Wrong place, wrong time," she muttered through damaged lips, the broken teeth catching on the broken skin.

"LIAR!" the second man yelled back, far too close to her face. His breath stank as if he hadn't cleaned his teeth in a year. "LIAR BITCH!"

"I know nothing that I haven't told you."

A right-handed punch slammed into her midriff and she tried to double over, winded, but couldn't as they'd tied her to a heavy wooden chair. She gasped for air, moaning, stars exploding in her head and not able to block out the pain that made her want to pass out. Anything to stop the hurt.

"We told you yesterday that this was your last chance. Now try to help." It was Scar-face again, the voice of reason.

"Or we'll fucking kill you right now!" yelled Bad Breath. "You are a filthy rebel whore, and I love killing fucking rebel whores!"

She found her breath, whimpering. "I really, really know nothing to help you," she said so softly that it was almost inaudible.

Bad Breath hit her again, this time full in the face and so hard that the chair toppled over, bouncing her onto her side. A foot caught her in the solar plexus, exposed as she couldn't ball-up, breathing became impossible and the men started targeting the area, professionals in pain.

"Last chance," Scar-face snarled, bending over her.

She was almost unconscious, tried to mutter something but didn't even know what she said to them, and they probably couldn't understand any of it between the tears, the gasped oxygen and the broken mouth.

They returned to the kicking game, but now it was indiscriminate. They had given up on their hope to get something meaningful from her, so now they just enjoyed what they did for a job. Boot after boot rained in, and another one of her ribs cracked causing a new world of pain, a new shriek of terror and the world started to fade away. They kept kicking until suddenly Bad Breath realised that she was out, unconscious.

"Leave her," he said. "We maybe give her one more go later, but either she knows nothing, or she'll take her secrets to the grave."

"Perhaps she is telling the truth?"

"I somehow doubt that."

Nobby Small looked from their mountain perch over the border in to Syria through a pair of high power binoculars. The place reminded him of the mountainous territory between Oman and the United Arab Emirates, a place he'd spent most of last year training local forces. The land was harsh, the few animals found there mainly limited to poisonous snakes and equally poisonous scorpions, and the temperatures were not designed for humans.

He'd been ten years with the Regiment and made the rank of Sergeant. How many bullets had somehow missed his body in that time he didn't wish to contemplate.

"It's a bastard of a place Nobby," Chippy Woods voice sounded behind him. "A bloody worrying place for Pete Davies to be stuck."

"Why the fuck do we get involved in these bloody places? We seem to solve one and get caught in another," he replied to the Admin Sergeant Major.

"Aye, you're right," Chippy responded. "But don't let the Boss hear you saying that."

"Do you think they'll send us over the border?" Nobby asked. "It's not too far to get to Damascus, and we could help the lad there much better than from up here."

"Never say never."

"And who cares who wins," Nobby added, making a mockery of the SAS motto.

"The sad thing is, you and I do, me old mucker," Chippy told him. "That's why we keep coming back when we could have walked into a job in personal security for some of those celebrity ladies last year."

Nobby had picked out a couple of Syrian ladies about a mile off in his binos. "And I guess they would have been a wee bit better looking than these lasses over here."

"But they're just like big birds," the Sergeant Major said.

"What do you mean by that?" asked Nobby, walking in to the trap.

"They've all had a Cockatoo."

They had decided to go in at midnight at Jack's insistence, Pete preferring to wait until at least two in the morning when the minority of soldiers would be on duty, and those that were would be at their lowest level of concentration. He knew that there was a good likelihood that Lilia was dead and if not, in a condition where she would never be the same again. A few additional hours would not make any difference.

Jack felt every hour counted and would have even hit the place in broad daylight. His soldiering skills were being badly affected by his emotions.

The car was ready — fuelled up as best they could, engine looking good with oil and water levels checked. Their guns were ready. Grenades cleaned. Ahmed wanted to go in with them, as did young Jaf, but Pete had talked them out of it, at least the attack on the building. Their job would be diversions.

They had three hours to wait. Pete ate, Jack fretted.

Time stood still.

Chapter Twenty-Four

2nd September 2013, Damascus, Syria

She was walking barefoot in calf-length grass, up a slight incline. It had to be Spring, the dandelions, daisies and buttercups adding colour to the lush green mat of the meadow. She wore a long, white satin dress that came down almost to where the grass brushed against her lower legs, a white lacy headscarf around her long hair.

She was going to get married.

Continuing onwards up the hill, she could make out a figure on the summit, sitting down and facing away from her. At this range it was impossible to tell if it was male or female, but she felt no threat from it and knew this is where she had to go.

Drawing closer, she could, at last, see it was a man, his back tanned from the sun, muscular, but lean. He was squatted down in a yoga-like position, legs folded beneath him, an Australian bush hat on his head.

From fifteen feet away she realised it was her husband, Christopher. He wasn't dead after all.

"Chris," she called.

The man turned to face her. It wasn't Chris, it was Jack. And in the centre of his forehead was a clean, round entry hole of a bullet. The body toppled over sideways.

"NOOOO!" she screamed, waking herself.

She lay panting on the cell floor. "No," she whispered. "No, no, no," she muttered, drifting back into unconsciousness.

Her eyes were almost glued shut from the swelling added to the mucus and blood that had seeped into them due to damage from the beatings. The left one was the worst — possibly because most of the big punches had been right-handers from the men. She was lying on the floor, free from the chair, not daring to move as it hurt too much. When she did move, she had to break herself free from the gunk on the floor. Gunk that had once been her blood and her bodily fluids. She thought that maybe her lower left rib was broken, the pain there was so great.

Her mind drifted to the dream. Had she really seen Jack dead, or was this an hallucination? She also remembered another vision of a beach, but she was pretty sure that was just her mind falling to pieces. But had Jack been there, at least in some form?

She wasn't sure. Dream and reality were a blurred mix.

She didn't think she could take much more. The next time might be the last. Another good kicking would probably be the end of her.

She tried not to think of escape and the outside world, of England, of Jack, of sunshine. She knew that in all probability she would never see any of these things again.

But every time she drifted off, visions would return, further confusing the truth.

"How do we handle this?" asked Bad Breath. "She's passing out sooner than before, so she doesn't have much left."

"I think she has nothing to tell us," Scar-face told him. "She's taken a lot, especially for a woman."

"We do what we are paid for and try and get some information out of her. If it means using the soldiers to scare her more, then we do that as well."

"I bloody hate that stuff. Some of those bastards are not human."

"Can they get an answer though, or must we try again?"

Scar-face sighed, shaking his head. "Before you say it again, I know it's my job, but I bloody hate beating up women. Bloody rebel terrorists I couldn't care less about, but women…"

Bad Breath was silent for a moment. "We leave it an hour or two, get a bit of food and sleep. No-one senior will be here before morning, so no-one pushing us. Then we have a last try." He scratched the stubble on his chin. "If we fail, the boys get a chance. It will probably kill her anyway."

"At least it will be over for her."

"That's true."

The Rover was parked in shadows, away from the main buildings. In typical military fashion, Pete went through the plan again, highlighting how they would handle various situations if they occurred. It was what he had been taught since he'd joined the army, and with the Regiment it was second nature. He wasn't happy with it: it was too early for him — the hours between two and four would be better — and they didn't have enough people or firepower, they were too far from the safety of the border, and Assad had troops everywhere between where they were and that safety.

It would be a straightforward dash for freedom. He thought of the possibilities: capture, torture, death.

It was just after twelve, and Pete was trying to eke out every additional minute he could. The more people not awake, the easier it would be. In, grab Lilia, out and run. Of course they could only grab her if she was there, if they found her...

Too many 'ifs' for SAS planning.

Earlier both he and Jack had spoken to Colin, letting him know the plan. The MI6 man called it 'suicide', imploring them to reconsider. They had refused, and despite his reservations, he knew he would have tried to save the girl. He had passed the details on to the SAS men on the border, along with the planned route out. They promised to do their best to assist.

Colin had also asked London if they could maybe use an airstrike, perhaps not with a manned aircraft, but maybe a drone armed with hellfire missiles. With support like this the men on the ground would have a better chance...

The request was refused. The team were a deniable asset.

"So, I guess we're as ready as we'll ever be," Jack told the other three in the car. "Let's do it."

"One last time," Pete interrupted. "Ahmed. Where do you go after you leave the vehicle?"

Jack put his head in his hands but remained silent.

Pete ignored him and continued running though the plan.

Bad Breath shook Scar-face into wakefulness, the guy somehow sleeping on the rock-hard mattresses the army issued them when on duty here. He had hardly slept at all, unable to get comfortable, and wished he was home. Not to see his wife of course: she was too old and ugly, fat from the six kids they'd had over the last eight years. He just wanted to be in the local tavern drinking some rough aniseed drink and ogling at the twenty-year-old barmaid. It was said by some of the lads that she was a game girl after a few beers.

"What time is it?" Scar-face slurred, still in never-never land.

"Just gone twelve-thirty. I thought we should get on with things."

The half-asleep soldier swung his legs off the side of the bed, rubbing his eyes with the palms of his hands. "Fuck. I was dreaming about my wife," he told the older man. "Just about to do the dirty deed, then you wake me up."

"Wait until you're a few more years married," Bad Breath said. "You'll dream about anybody except her then."

"We'll see." He pulled himself off the bed and staggered forward a step, still dazed. "I just need a piss and a wash, then I'll be right with you."

"I'll pour two coffees, then we get on with it."

Ahmed had no watch, so they didn't synchronise the time. Pete thought it simpler to use Ahmed's diversion as the zero hour, then take it from there. Simplicity was the key to everything: the more complex they made things, the more room for error.

Jaf was at the entrance to the square where the fuel bowsers were parked up. He would whistle if someone came, then leg it, every man for himself.

A grenade sat comfortably in each of Ahmed's palms, the pins already worked loose to make the final extraction easier. He found a point where three fuel trucks were parked next to each other and climbed up a metal ladder that was fixed to the middle one. He slid along the upper surface, keeping low to the vehicle to stop his silhouette showing. This wasn't the first time he'd blown up a fuel bowser, so he knew where he was going, and soon reached his goal, a metal circular lid about halfway down the tank. He flipped a catch and opened it, dangling his arm in to the space. The tank was full, and he pulled out his arm, stinking of aviation fuel.

He closed the lid again, then climbed down from the lorry. He would normally do the same test to the other two trucks, but this time he wasn't too bothered about the amount of petrol he destroyed, mainly about the size of the bang. This would do fine.

He moved along the side of the vehicle to where the truck's own fuel tank was. Here he found a good place to wedge the two grenades.

He eyed the distance to the exit of the yard and the cover of the buildings. He would have about seven seconds from when he pulled the pins and let the spring loaded arms slam over. He reckoned he could be behind the first cover in five. Close, but okay.

With the index finger of each hand, he pulled out the split pins, holding the arm next to the grenade body. He checked his route out again, looked at the space he had selected for the tiny charges.

He rammed them in to the space above the petrol tank, released his fingers and ran like hell.

"What took you so long? Been standing here for bloody ages."

"Couldn't get the picture of my wife out of my head…"

"Stop! No more details. Come on let's get the bitch."

Somewhere, far away, Lilia could hear the sound of footsteps on hard sand. She was on a beach in Spain, eyes closed to block out the sun, skin hot and moist. The steps became louder, then she could hear the sound of a key turning in a door, the light intensifying. What was happening?

She forced open her one good eye and reality flooded back. Fear released the contents of her bladder, the urine joining the rest of the mess on the cell floor.

"No, please no," she muttered through lips that looked like sausages. "I know nothing."

Thunder sounded from somewhere outside, interrupting her pleas. She was slipping back under again, escaping from the fear and pain.

The boy had done good Pete thought, eyeing the thirty yards between them and the door. The sky was red with fire, the whole place no doubt awake, but also no doubt confused and in panic. He was rising out of their hiding place.

"Go! Go! Go!" he cried, nervous energy coursing through his veins. "Let's go!"

Jack was up. Both had AK47s on their right arms, magazines in place and each with a second clip taped to the first one, but upside down, ready to release the empty mag and reverse it for thirty more bullets. As yet no targets, and the door was still just yards away.

"We shoot out the lock," Pete yelled. "Keep back!"

Just at that second the door swung open, Assad troops spilling into the opening to investigate the explosion. Pete hit them with three bursts, two to three rounds each. At that range it was like taking candy from a baby, and they collapsed to the ground, dead and dying. Pete didn't stop, hurdling the bodies, Jack a yard behind.

"Watch our backs!" Pete yelled.

Jack turned as a door opened close to the entrance they'd bulldozed through. Two men — half-asleep and one in boxers — came out. Jack opened up, a stream of about ten rounds that ended up partly in the soldiers and partway up the walls around them.

"Try shorter bursts!" Pete hollered. "Not sure how many we have to take out."

Up ahead two unarmed men emerged from a door on the right of the corridor, both looking bemused. One looked like he'd seen action and not come out of it particularly well. Pete fired two more bursts and one went down, the ugly one catching a round in the leg and hanging off the wall. In seconds Pete was on him.

"We're looking for a lady," he hollered, grabbing the man by the throat. He kicked out the man's legs, dropping him to the floor like a sack of spuds. The guy screamed from the pressure this put on his wound.

Jack surged past him and turned into the cell.

Pete's voice was in the dream now, far away, not real. Her mind was getting used to the false visions now, the dying hopes. She tried to let the darkness in, but the cries from outside the cell persisted.

What was happening? Could this be a trick?

Through her half-sealed left eye, she saw another shape enter the room and she cowered into the corner, waiting for a boot. "No... please leave me..."

She heard a voice that she thought was Jack. Impossible, he was dead: she must be dead.

A gentle hand rested on her shoulder, reassuring words washed over her. "Jack?"

She passed out.

"She's here Pete," Jack screamed. "Still alive."

Pete entered the cell, taking in the mess, the smell, the condition of the girl. "Pick her up. We need to get out right now."

"She's in a horrible state," Jack said. "If we move her she could die."

"If she stays here, she will die. Get her! Now!"

Pete was back in the corridor, releasing three-round bursts in each direction to keep people out of the way.

The way they came in was slightly further away than the other exit door down the corridor, but it was open and the car was nearer. "Are you ready?"

Jack emerged, Lilia, in a fireman's lift, hanging unconscious from his left shoulder. His right arm was free for the AK. "Ready."

They hurried quickly back down the passage, Pete leading. He fired rounds in to a few of the other cell doors, shattering their locks.

Jaf was by the Rover and Ahmed was about a dozen yards off, looking in the direction of the gunfire. He thought the man and the lady were probably dead, the whole night a bad dream. Troops were heading in the direction of the burning fuel yard, assuming that was the main target. He wondered how much longer Jaf and himself should hang around before they took responsibility for their own lives. Things were soon going to get out of hand, and he wasn't ready to die just yet.

"Look!"

It was Jaf, leaving his position by the car, just behind him, his finger pointing.

He followed it.

Pete and Jack were running towards them and Jack had something on his back. It didn't look very much like a person. He feared the worst.

"Get to the car!" he ordered the boy.

Jack was exhausted, the energy he'd found from the adrenalin of action long gone. Lilia, though a woman, was a dead weight. She moaned something, but he had no clue as to what she was saying. At least she was alive.

"Get to the Rover!" Pete screamed as he saw the kids. "We need to hurry."

Thirty seconds later they were there.

"Jaf, get in the back door. Jack, you and Lilia on the back seat, do what you can with her. Ahmed, front with me. I need you to guide me and ride shotgun. Anyone in the way we shoot. Questions later."

They followed his instructions swiftly, Ahmed with an AK47 in his hand and the window down.

It was now a race for freedom.

Chapter Twenty-Five

2nd September 2013, the Lebanese border

Colin was with the Colonel, his ear to the secure phone. Jack was on the other end.

"We're driving through the city now, and it seems that government forces haven't sussed-out what is going on yet," he heard in his ear. "We will have to try and bash our way through any check-points: we can't bluff our way anymore, not with Lilia looking like this."

"Is she OK?" Colin asked, wondering immediately how stupid the comment must sound at the other end.

"Dreadful beating, broken teeth, I think a couple of bust ribs, which means possible internal organ damage." He paused, trying to remain unemotional, failing for a second before regaining his composure. "She's breathing alone, and I'm using what I can to try and reduce the swelling to the face, especially around the eyes. Legs and arms seem intact, so if needed I think she can walk."

"You've done a great job Jack, now just get the team out. We're waiting for you at the border."

The Colonel muscled in. "Can I chat to my man?"

Colin handed the phone over and Jack passed his forward to Pete.

"You OK Pete?" the military man enquired.

"Driving without hands-free Boss, but other than that, having a ball."

The Colonel smiled grimly, imagining the stress levels they were all suffering. "What armaments do you have with you?"

"We have four AKs and enough rounds from the rebel lad with us to have a shoot-out in Dodge City, a few grenades left and two RPGs. That's about it. Oh, and two nine-mil pistols."

"How long to the border?"

"With no hostiles, about thirty minutes, but can't see that lasting forever."

"Foot to the floor Pete, foot to the floor."

Following the break-out, the area of the airport was in chaos. Reports filtered to the local commander of a major rebel assault on the fuel depot, of a platoon storming the interrogation centre and releasing the inmates there. Troops were first directed to the fuel storage area, only to find no-one there, just a bunch of burning lorries.

His driver pulled up outside the prisoner cell block and he went inside. Bodies littered the corridors, most dead but some crying in pain. He stepped over the dead and tried to get the story out of the living. At the far end of the hall he found one of the jailers, a tourniquet strapped around the top of his thigh, with a medic standing over him preparing the morphine.

"What happened?"

The man's face was white with shock and pain, a scar running down one side. He grimaced as the needle broke the skin.

"Two men, armed with Kalashnikovs, shot their way up the corridor. They took the girl with them."

"Which girl?"

"The one we were questioning. The one who was found with the rebels."

The Major had heard about this woman, but never met her. "Did they take any other prisoners?"

"No, just shot the locks off the other doors, then the freed rebels... released the rest."

So the target had been the woman, the Major surmised. The rest were just to further confuse the situation. Why?

"Set up road blocks around the area," he ordered a Sergeant. "I need to get on the radio to HQ. They need to know what's happening here."

He headed back to his command post and a call he didn't really want to make.

They were skirting around the southern edge of the city, deciding to stick to main roads to make the best time. It was clear that the confusion couldn't last forever, and the further away from the action they were, the better for them.

Pete drove, Lilia slept. Jack had calmed her down and given her a light painkiller, avoiding anything strong in case they had to leave the car. Ahmed stared through the dusty windscreen, trying to spot problems before they materialised and guiding Pete, while Jaf watched for signs of pursuit. It was ten minutes since they'd left the airport and the honeymoon couldn't last.

"The next road is the Damascus-Beirut Highway," Ahmed told Pete. "About twenty minutes to the border I'm told."

Pete acknowledged the information by pressing harder on the accelerator, pushing their speed still higher. "Twenty minutes to a good pint of beer," he told Ahmed. "Maybe I buy one for you too, despite your age."

"Roadblocks at all major crossing points with Lebanon," the General ordered over the phone. "It's the nearest border, so quite probably where they will run to."

"Just had a report of a pale coloured 4x4 leaving the area soon after the attack Sir," the Major told him. Information was coming in constantly now, some making sense and some not. "Seems it may be related to the attack. Three or four men inside."

"They'll try for Beirut," the General said, mainly to himself. "Block the border post. All troops in the area to assemble there. Hurry!"

"There's a lot of lights further back on the road," Jaf reported. Jack looked back. Too many for normal traffic. The chase was on.

"Looks like they're after us," he told all that wanted to listen.

Pete had already clocked the lights in the rear mirror. They didn't bother him: those behind he could outrun. What was happening up front was more of a worry...

The Colonel was summoned to where Nobby was, now using Night Vision Goggles, tracking things about two miles away at the main road border post. They gave a pale green glow to his face. "Think you should see this Boss," he said.

The senior man took the NVGs and adjusted the field of vision until he found the border. Through the goggles he could see troop movements, towards what looked like defensive positions. Hard to fix the number, but he'd guess about twenty men. Just then a truck drew up and another ten men jumped off the tailgate.

"About thirty men there with the new lot," Nobby confirmed, using a second set of NVGs that he'd fired up. "Looks like they're going to wait for them and hope they go for broke by the main road."

Colin had joined them. "They haven't got a hope," he said. "Look at the lights down the road. Looks like they are either chasing someone or trying to get reinforcements out there fast."

The Colonel moved his goggles down the road, but the lights flared out the optics. "Caught between a rock and a hard place," he said. Nobby moved to straight forward binos and held his focus for about a minute.

"Looks like a pale coloured car between the two groups, coming this way. Too far to be sure."

"The Rover was once white," Colin said grimly. "Shit! Not much we can do. No permission to cross the border."

"I don't need permission," said the Boss. "Get the men mounted up Sergeant Major. We're going in."

The Lieutenant Colonel at the border post surveyed his line of soldiers. They were armed with automatic rifles and Kalashnikovs, no anti-tank weaponry, but more than enough to stop a car. He knew more troops were routing out of the city as he assembled his people, so his main concern right now was a friendly fire incident. Most of these men were border guards, but he'd also dragged in cooks and engineers, not top class soldiers.

"Keep them calm Sergeant Major. These guys are not elite troops."

"OK Sir. Understood." He moved off to spread the word, settling the young men down.

"Sergeant," the officer said. "Get the barriers put down. I know it will stop nothing, but it will look as though the place is closed down for business."

The man went away with two privates. The Colonel hoped the reinforcements would arrive before the rebels did. Alternatively he hoped that the rebels weren't actually coming at all.

"The border post we bypassed, on the way in, must be about three to five miles off," Pete told the car's occupants. "Could be where they'll try and hit us."

"We have three weapons at the ready," Ahmed said.

"Four," young Jaf said. "I can fire a pistol."

"Five," said a muffled voice. "If I'm going to die, I'm going to die fighting," Lilia told them.

"Good to have you back on board," Pete said with a wry grin, glancing in the rear-view mirror.

"Even better for me," Jack added, smiling down at her.

The SAS Land Rovers crossed the Lebanese border into no-man's-land, the troops ready for action, weapons cocked. They had to hurry — their mate was about to enter a death zone and only they could influence the outcome.

145

Colin, the Colonel and a radio man watched from a point on the border where they could see the whole situation unfolding, and the Boss kept the SAS men up-to-date.

"Assad forces are manning-up the border post," Colin told Jack over the secure phone. "You also appear to have a tail, so no time to stop."

"We've noticed the lights. You're suggesting we just try and smash through the defences. This was our rough plan."

"We believe it is the only way to play it Jack," Colin told him. "The SAS boys are heading down there now but may get there a little too late."

"At least they'll be there if we get through. Means they can stop the chasers coming with us."

"God speed and good luck."

Chapter Twenty-Six

2nd September 2013, Jdaidit Yabws Border Post

The Syrian troops could now see the light coloured 4x4 coming towards them and showing no intent to stop.

"Should we signal them to pull over, Sir?" a Sergeant asked.

"I think it would make no difference," the senior officer told him. "We'll wait until they are closer and then open fire. We must stop the car. If the occupants die, so be it, but I'd like to catch at least one of them to find out who they are and what they were doing in Damascus."

"Just give the word, Sir. The troops are as ready as they'll ever be."

They could see the border post now, see that the barriers were closed, couldn't see any sign of human activity.

The car hurtled forward, no reduction in speed.

"Can't see the soldiers, but Colin says they are there," Pete said. "Expect incoming rounds anytime now." His face was set, his knuckles white from his tense grip on the steering wheel. "Good luck everyone."

The Lieutenant Colonel spoke softly into the Sergeant Major's ear. "It's your show now. Fire when you think it's best."

The Senior NCO nodded and stood, his focus on the approaching vehicle. "OK lads, we open up any time now. Just aim at the car. Every hit counts. On my word we fire."

He paused, counting the yards between him and the Rover. It was about five hundred and closing quickly. He fought off the temptation to hit the button now, waiting the additional seconds that brought the range down to about one hundred meters.

"FIRE!"

The SAS men heard the gunfire above their screaming engines, knew that they were arriving too late. When they rounded the next corner the buildings would be in view, but that was still about thirty seconds away.

They charged on, flicking off safety catches.

The first rounds all somehow missed the Rover, nerves and a fast moving vehicle getting the better of the second-line troops that formed the ambush. The tense occupants of the vehicle all saw the muzzle flashes, and Pete started weaving at high speed to try and make the target harder to hit. They seemed to be living a charmed life.

"Hold tight!" he yelled.

The second flashes were marked by a shattered windshield and the sound like rocks hitting the car. The screen was a mess of cracks and Pete leant forward and punched it, a shower of glass blowing back on to him and into the rear of the vehicle.

They were about a hundred and fifty feet from the first barriers.

More flashes, and Pete lost control of the Rover.

No-one in the defensive line knew who'd fired the shot, and none of them really cared. They also didn't know it had hit a front tyre that shredded quickly due to the pace the car was travelling at.

They cheered though when the car seemed to dig in its nose and tip over and over, rolling to within sixty-five feet of their line. There it stopped, steam coming from the engine area and black smoke from the destroyed wheel. They stopped firing and, when their applause petered out, there was a deathly silence.

"Keep your eyes on the vehicle men!" the Sergeant Major instructed. "Do not fire until I tell you. We would like the pigs inside alive, if any of them still are."

Inside the car, Pete was first to react.

"Quiet guys," he whispered. "They probably think we're all dead. How are we all?"

Jaf answered in a high-pitched voice, obviously in a state of shock. "OK."

Jack had Lilia in his arms, blood leaking from a cut on his forehead. "Lilia's out again but breathing. I'm OK."

Nothing from Ahmed. Pete leant across. The boy was dead, probably the bullet that had taken out the windscreen. He told the others.

The car had stopped, rolling on its side, the battered roof facing the attackers, so no-one could see them yet. Pete knew that it would provide no cover at all if the bullets started flying, but right now it had the troops guessing as to the condition of the occupants.

"OK guys," he said. I'm going to try and get a look out there through the windscreen. Keep quiet and let's see."

He edged carefully forward, knees crunching shattered glass.

The warriors that had once been non-combatants basked in the afterglow of their battle success, ears ringing from the sound of their weapons, bullets detonating and working parts slamming backwards and forwards. Smiles on every face, back-slapping one another, a task well done. It was not the reaction of professional soldiers, but these weren't that.

Even the true soldiers amongst them lowered their guards.

It would prove a costly mistake.

The four SAS open-top Rovers glided in with engines off, turning side on a hundred and fifty feet to the rear of the Assad force. The soldiers on board knew their approximate arcs of fire from the position of the vehicle, something they'd practiced a million times on exercises in the Brecon Beacons. These were no amateurs, and their lives depended on their smooth drill and conditioned reflexes.

They opened up on the men in front of them. The Syrians had no chance.

"Time to go," Pete shouted into the car. "The Cavalry just turned up."

He began to assist Jack in moving Lilia out of the front window, trying to protect her from further injury. Jaf climbed over the back of the rear seat and tried to help. She moaned, but did not come back round, probably a good thing Pete believed.

The firing had again ceased, and he helped Jack get Lilia on to his shoulder.

"Go forward slowly," he told him. "Keep your arms up or out to the side."

He ducked back in to the car.

"What are you doing?" Jaf asked.

"I want to take Ahmed out. He deserves a decent burial."

The first cars from the chasing pack were only a couple of hundred yards from the border post and could see that all was not well. They stopped, troops dismounted and took up firing positions from rock and bush cover. Binoculars and NVGs scanned the area.

"They're getting away," someone shouted.

"Open fire!"

Jack, Lilia and Jaf were rounding a barrier, the SAS men already acknowledging their presence. A few of the troops came forward to help, one a certified field medic. Lilia was helped onto a stretcher and a shot of pain-relief was injected after a rapid assessment of her condition. The group headed for the SAS vehicles.

Somewhere in the distance, the sound of a helicopter could be heard.

Pete noticed the trucks and APCs too late. He dived for the cover of the Rover engine block just as the first hail of lead peppered the ground around him. He glanced back at the SAS soldiers, his colleagues, another hundred yards of open ground away. Impossible.

An RPG launcher lay next to the vehicle, spilled out during the crash. His AK47 was slung across his back.

He pulled the cell phone out of his pocket, but the display was smashed and the button failed to bring any results when pressed. He threw it onto the tarmac.

Nobby Small was looking from the shelter of the buildings that formed the Syrian border. He indicated he would join Pete, but both of them knew it was a suicide mission. Rounds fell all around the vehicle.

"Get back!" Pete shouted. "I'll put down some fire and withdraw. You can't be here."

The mission was not official, the SAS should not be on Syrian soil, and the odds were probably against them. An APC started to move towards the car crash, its machine gun hammering out bullets. It was time to do or die.

Pete calmly prepared the RPG, ignoring the death that was hitting the floor only inches away. It was a single chance, and he had to make it work. He felt sick but focused on the task at hand. Nobby was firing his rifle at the armoured vehicle, the rounds pinging off it.

Pete took a deep breath and rolled out of the cover, just enough to get the shot. He steadied his breathing, sighted the weapon and pressed the trigger.

The rocket propelled grenade hissed out of the launcher, roaring towards the APC. Pete didn't stay to watch, jumping up and running for the safety of the border.

He managed to get to twenty-five feet from safety when a round hit him in the back. He was dead before he hit the ground.

Nobby made it to the Rovers with Pete's body over his shoulder. Blood ran down the side of his right leg where a round had grazed him.

"He's dead, but I'm not leaving him here," he told the others grimly. "He deserves better."

The Sergeant Major ordered the vehicles out, and they charged off in the direction they had come, one of their own finished.

The Syrian Air Force helicopter hovered just east of the border post above Syrian soil. In the confusion it had been called out too late. If summoned at the beginning of the chase, the result would have been very different.

Suspended there above the border, guns pointing in to Lebanon, the pilot awaited orders.

"Break off pursuit."

The pilot watched the convoy carve its way in to Lebanon, kicked the right pedal and spun away back towards Damascus.

Chapter Twenty-Seven

21st September 2013, Hereford, UK

The mood was sombre at the SAS barracks at Hereford. The group of mainly special-forces soldiers stood at a small clock tower in the safety of the lines. The only outsiders were Jack, Lilia, Colin and Jaf.

Some were in uniform, including Jack, most in jeans and polo shirts, sports clothing, and suits. They had come to pay their respects to a brother-in-arms.

The side of the tower displayed the names of the members of the SAS who hadn't made it back: from a war, a campaign, a crisis situation, from somewhere in the world. In their forces jargon, the names had failed to 'beat the clock'. Today a new name was added to the list, a certain Captain Peter Davies. It was just a name: no explanation of where or how, no citation to brag of his bravery.

Few tears were shed — only Colin, Jaf and Lilia had a weak moment.

This was how warriors left the world.

The ones who lived on went for a drink and a memory. It could be their turn next.

"So we failed," Lilia said to the people at the table. "Al Assad lives on, the regime is still killing people, millions have lost their homes and their country."

"It was an impossible task from the start," Colin told them. "We set ourselves a goal that was just too big for us."

"And it cost Pete his life," the girl added. "I feel such a failure."

"It cost you a great deal too," Jack told her. He didn't go in to detail about the two fractured ribs, the scars and stitches that had been needed to repair her body, the dental work that was still in progress to allow her to eat properly again.

"You only failed if you stop now," Jaf said. They all looked at him.

"No-one is going back there," Colin told them. "It was almost suicide last time. To do it again would be more than stupid."

"No-one has to go back in," the boy informed them, showing a wisdom above his years. "You must stop this war from here. From UK. From Europe."

The adults looked at the child, then at one another. A boy barely eleven years of age was giving them direction, a new reason for living.

They nodded in agreement. A pact was made.

"For Pete," they toasted.

Epilogue

14th March 2014, London

Speakers For Syria was a lobby group formed to be the voice of the people of an oppressed country. They somehow picked up on the Lilia story soon after her return from Syria, but stood off until the teams of doctors, plastic surgeons and dentists had completed their initial efforts to fix a broken woman. Some said that Colin had 'accidentally' leaked her details, knowing that involvement in something would be a good therapy, speeding along the healing process.

Details of the military part of the operation were kept quiet.

Jack didn't care who had passed her name: the new 'hobby' was certainly therapeutic, and he could see, better than most, the improvements in her confidence, the change in her mindset. As soon as she was ready, he had proposed marriage, and she'd immediately accepted.

At first she had only attended meetings, helping others understand the problems within the country. Soon though she also was attending the conferences and presentations, firstly within the UK, but then also in Europe. But as her internal and external scars healed, she was asked to speak herself, first to small gatherings in London, but then to larger groups around the country.

When the official refugee figure passed the million mark, Lilia offered her services wherever Speakers for Syria needed her. One million countrymen and women homeless, and that was only the recorded number. How many rich used their wealth to escape, and how many had crossed borders illegally and made a new life? How many had died in the attempt?

For Lilia it was an easy decision to make: to help however she could.

Lilia stepped up onto the stage, the scars on her face fading but still very evident. The dental work was wonderful, her smile a beam of light. Jack thought he'd die: he felt this way every time his wife spoke in public.

"Thank you for your welcome," Lilia started, scanning the crowd in the hall, partly as a time grabber to calm her nerves and partly to try and spot hostile faces in the assembled masses.

"We've come a long way since I was saved from imprisonment in Damascus. We have been accepted by the Swedish government only this week as the official face of protest against the wrongdoings of Mr Bashir Al Assad. We can add this to our success in campaigns in the UK, Ireland and Norway, with others already voicing unofficial support. We are winning the international support needed to force the military regime in Syria out of power.

"Exact figures are hard to come by, estimations are that over three million people from my country have been made homeless, many of them fleeing the regime and their country. With these people we also lose some of our core skills, our workforce. How should we fix our industries, our services, if we have no professionals to do the work? But we must.

"All of us here are the future of Syria. We are what will fix the country, whether we are Syrians or not. I am sure that you all wish to be part of the resurrection of a beautiful land, not just our home grown experts. We need everyone."

She gestured to the crowd, a wide hand wave to encapsulate them all. Her face was serious, a strong voice passed the message.

"I hope you all — I beg you all — to support our cause. We are winning worldwide, but we are not winning in the most important place." A pause. "My home."

The crowd clapped in their appreciation and support.

Jack smiled to himself as he joined the cheering. She had become a highly skilled orator.

Moscow, Russia, 1st April 2014

"And so I implore you to support our cause Mister President. I know that your country and my country, Syria, have long ties. I also know that friction with the Western World can sometimes cloud both our judgments, Britain — my new home — and Russia, but some things are far more important than winning a set in a political tennis match.

"Please join the alliance to force Mister Assad to step down and do the right thing. To place his land ahead of his ambitions. To allow free and open talks without violence. To tempt the refugees of Syria to return to their homes and make it a place that foreigners want to come to. If you use your influence, if you tell him no more arms, no guns, bullets, missiles; no food aid, money, safe havens, then he must listen. Surely you can see this."

Lilia paused in her delivery, only ten seconds but letting the silence stretch. She turned her head as if in contemplation so that the scarred left side of her face was visible to the crowd. She returned to eye contact.

"With your support this war is over. It has no heart. The brain is starved of oxygen and Assad is forced to make the decision he is so terrified of. A Syria without the Al Assad government having free rein."

She looked over to the Russian President, daring him to return the stare. He did. Not what she had hoped for. She tried another track, something unplanned.

"Russia was once a monster. It ruled its people with fear. It was called Communism." She was still watching the Russian leader, looking for the tiniest reaction. He was a bloody good poker player. Nothing showed.

"Russia today is an oil economy, a mining nation, a major player in the capitalist world. Your companies are leaders by example of what can be possible. Your people are free thinkers."

She swept her gaze over the mainly Russian audience.

A nervous tension was in the air.

"If your country can do this in a few short years, why can my country not? If you are their friend, why can't you guide them? Are you leaders, or are you followers?" Her gaze returned to the President, a hard challenging glare. "Please help your friends in Syria. Guide them out of this madness."

The leader's face hadn't altered all the way through the exchange. She guessed she'd lost this battle.

"Thank you all for your time. I'd like to hand the stage over to my colleague, Julia Humble, who will take us through the economics of the crisis."

She was standing with Jack at the drinks reception at the end of the presentations, a glass of champagne in a hand that still shook.

"You'd think after all the speeches I've made that I wouldn't get so bloody nervous anymore," she whispered to him.

"I think the nerves are just because of the passion you feel for your cause."

"I know you're right, but it doesn't make me feel better. I lost today."

A man in a dark lounge suit approached them where they were standing, Jack noticing he had an earpiece tucked into his right ear. Security. He stopped in front of them.

"Would you be kind enough to follow me," he asked in Russian accented English. "Someone would like to meet you."

"Who would that be?" asked Jack.

"Afraid I cannot answer that question, Sir."

They followed the man out of the reception and down a corridor until they came to a door with another dark-suited man standing in front of it. Their guide produced his ID and was given access. They entered a large high-ceilinged and well-decorated room. Leaning against a large mahogany desk was the Russian President.

"So pleased you accepted the invitation," he said. "Another champagne? Maybe a Pol Roger, something more in tune with the British." They understood his comment was a reference to a certain late Mister Churchill who had sworn by the bubbly fluid. Was this a good or bad sign?

"Thank you," Lilia responded, Jack still pondering.

Glasses were brought over, the drinks poured, and the Russian toasted the two Brits. "You spoke very well today," he said. "Put me on the spot a little in front of all the media." He raised his glass again, another small sip. "Well done."

"Thank you Sir. I try my best. It is the country of my birth."

"You also spoke well of Russia, perhaps better than we deserve. Not everything is so perfect here, and we also need support from the outside world from time to time. I appreciated that."

"I try and speak the truth Mister President. Nothing and nowhere is ever totally perfect."

The Russian leader turned to one of his men and made a signal. He again faced Lilia and Jack.

"I think we will have another toast, but this one more in line with my own taste." The man appeared with three glasses of frozen vodka, the outside of each glass coated in a thin layer of ice. "I will support your cause. I will talk to Bashir and try and persuade him it is a time for change." He raised his glass. "To a better and peaceful Syria!"

The news was all over the newspapers the next day, the Russian President pledging to use his influence to attempt to end the civil war in Syria, to assist in returning the refugees back to their homeland. He told international reporters assembled in Moscow that he finally felt that the estimated quarter of a million dead in the country was too many for him to sleep easily at night. He had to at least 'try' and use his influence to change things.

Lilia and Jack read the reports in the early papers as they sat in the business section of the British Airways jet returning to London.

"You told me yesterday that you had lost. If this is you losing, God knows what you can achieve if you win!"

She leaned across and kissed him briefly, smiling happily. She wasn't shaking anymore.

TO BE CONTINUED....

Please leave a review!

I love the feeling of finishing a book, completing a tale. For me it gives both negative and positive emotions: on the one hand, I can look forward to starting the next story, to dreaming up a whole new set of characters, new scenarios, trying to make all my new ideas sound believable.

The negative part comes because once you finish the fantasy side of writing, you need to take up the technical side – corrections, tidying the manuscript, cover design, book description, etc.

That's the hard bit.

I hope that you enjoyed *Syrian Shadow*, and also hope you can find time to give me some feedback by way of a review. Your words influence my books, so please let me know what you want to read, what you enjoyed. Good, honest opinions are worth gold!

Thanks for reading and please try the next one!

Next is an excerpt of the follow-up book to Syrian Shadow…

Slasher

Chapter One

Trafalgar Square, London

The protest was over, the crowd breaking up and dispersing, some to their homes, some to the nearest boozer. Jeremy was included in the latter group, moving away from Trafalgar Square and its lazy lions, towards the Wagon Wheel Inn.

The home-bound part of the gathering were mainly family people, descending down to the Tube or standing in the autumn sunshine waiting for a big red bus. Their placards were mainly broken up and pushed in to rubbish bins, the statements on them crushed in to balls of paper, meaningless nothings now. They had had their say, and now it was time to re-join their wives and kids, another quiet night at home in front of the goggle box.

The pub crowd consisted mainly of rabble rousers, joining in any demonstration just for the hell of it. Jeremy was a ring-leader, pulling in people that he knew from other demos, rent a crowd for the cost of a SMS. He was a big lad, a touch over six foot, a forty-two inch chest and bulging biceps, barbed-wire tattoos on both arms and around his neck. His hair was dyed blond and spiked short, his right eyebrow had three neat cuts from a cut-throat razor. The left side of his face was scarred from an old confrontation with a beer glass. The other guy had come off much worse though.

"Let's get in the Wagon," he yelled at his cronies. "I nicked a wallet out there, so first round's on me."

A small cheer came from the twenty odd people with him, a slap on the back from the man nearest. He smiled to himself. If everyone bought a beer that afternoon, that was twenty lagers coming his way…

As the double doors of the pub were flung open, the normal punters moved out of the way of the mob, sensing the danger they brought with them. Some left their drinks and these were swiftly scooped up and drained by the newcomers. People headed to the exit.

"It's Happy Hour!" Jeremy told the barman. "Everything is ten bob."

The eighteen year old student behind the bar looked around for support from the management but found he had been deserted. He decided it best not to argue; he didn't need a good hiding.

A skinny youth in a pair of Doc Martens, jeans and a string vest leant over the bar and took a cardboard box of smokey bacon crisps, ripping the lid open and chucking packets out in every direction. "If Jez is getting the beers, I just bought dinner!" he yelled.

One of the other ruffians hurdled the bar and passed out a bottle of vodka. It soon disappeared.

"Where's yer CCTV?" Jeremy asked the boy behind the bar, slamming his balled fist on to the counter. "Show me."

The youth opened a door at the rear of the bar, thinking of running for it. At the end of a corridor he spotted the landlord, but the man quickly made himself scarce. He opened a small cupboard and pointed at the recording equipment and a monitor.

"It's all in here mate," he told the thug.

Jeremy slapped him full in the face, open handed, sounding like a gunshot. "I'm not yer fucking mate, so just remember that," he told the boy.

The student held on to the wall, stunned by the attack. "Sorry," he mumbled through a thick lip, a trickle of blood running down his chin.

While Jeremy focused on the video recorder, the boy sidled off in the same direction the landlord had taken.

"Jez, what you doing?" a call came from the bar. "Come and have a beer."

"Just got somethin' to fix," he called back, grabbing the recorder with both hands and ripping it out of the cupboard, leads popping off the back. "Just be a sec."

He held the machine above his head, then threw it as hard as he could at the far wall. Some plastic parts exploded off it, but this wasn't good enough for Jeremy, so he slammed his steel toe-cap in to it, then crashed his heel on to the cassette housing on the top of the unit.

"Should do it," he told no-one in particular, returning to the bar.

Inside the room, furniture had been tossed around, the punters all gone. Beer and spirits were being consumed by the demonstrators at a fiendish rate.

"Drink what you can," Jez yelled. "We move in five minutes, before the pigs get organized."

He grabbed a bottle of whisky from one of the smaller lads in the pack, tipping it back. The liquor burned his throat, but he still swallowed quarter of the bottle.

"Pass me a beer," he asked a big ex-Hells Angel nick-named Chopper who was behind the bar.

He drained the glass of lager in a single gulp, hurling the mug at the wall. It smashed to pieces, showering the boys in that part of the room with fine glass splinters.

"OK," he called. "Let's get the fuck out of here. Next stop The Nelson."

Glasses shattered off the walls, unfinished drinks staining them. The mob headed for the door, some still hanging on to spirit bottles.

*

As they made their way to the next ale house, people crossed the road to avoid their progress. Those that didn't were pushed aside or knocked to the ground.

Coming around a corner at the bottom of Northumberland Avenue, Jeremy noticed another crowd had gathered, a man with a loud-hailer standing on a black plastic box holding their attention. He moved closer, wondering if they could have some fun there.

"What does our government care about Syria? What has been their reaction to over a million people having to flee their country? What have they given except rhetoric?" He paused for air, his breathing amplified through the still switched on device. "Would they have the same apathy if our country had large oil reserves, or a geographically important border?"

Jeremy's mob were by now on the edge of the gathering. He noted that the majority of the thirty odd people listening were women, all of them appearing to have Middle Eastern origins, some wearing full burka and black robes. He felt a rage building inside his head, the alcohol fuelling the madness. He started pushing through the crowd, his followers joining him.

The speaker saw the commotion beginning to his left and turned towards it. He fell silent, too late.

Jeremy kicked the box the man was standing on, causing the guy on it to stumble. He grabbed the man's arm, pulling him towards him, snatching the loud-hailer. He smashed the speaking end of the device on to the Syrians head, drawing blood.

"Who the fuck do you people think you are?" he bawled in to the mouthpiece. "This is my bloody country and you don't belong here, so stop bloody complaining about what we are doing for you. Piss off home and sort out your own shit!"

The crowd was backing off now, one of them helping the speaker who was still staggering from the blow with the hailer.

"I said piss off, and I mean now!" he shouted at them. "Guys. Speed them up!"

Some of the thugs started pushing the women to the ground, ripping at their robes. The men who helped the ladies were pushed to the floor and kicked. After a couple of minutes though, the thugs let them disperse.

No-one noticed the olive skinned man standing quietly by a lamppost just a few meters away.

*

They were on to their fourth pub, all about a mile or so apart, making it harder for the police to out-guess where they would hit next. The next one would be a ride on the Tube away to thoroughly mess up any theories the authorities may be forming.

Booze was all over the floor, as was the landlord who had been mad enough to stand up to them. He'd been smashed in the face then kicked repeatedly for his troubles, and now lay unconscious.

"Pass me the vodka," Jeremy called out. He was starting to feel drunk, but that was no reason to stop.

"Here Jez," a bottle was thrown his way, he fumbled it, but managed to stop it falling to the floor.

"Sack the juggler," some comedian yelled.

"Fuck off," grunted Jeremy, swigging from the bottle.

"Where next Jez?"

"How about the Horse at Waterloo?"

"Good idea. Puts a bit of distance between here and there."

"Let's roll!"

*

Jasim followed the mob at a safe distance. He didn't bother looking in to the pub they came out of: he'd already noted the results in the last two, so knew what to expect.

A Syrian from Damascus, he was also a devout Muslim. He'd lived in London for just over a year now, getting out of his country when things became too bad to stay. His parents had died in a car accident when he was sixteen, so he'd spent the last ten years looking after himself, getting money and food by hook or by crook. He stood six foot two in his socks, had a wiry rather than muscular frame, and had short cropped black hair and a stubbly beard. He'd learned over the time in England not to stand out too much as a follower of Islam.

He followed the crowd in to a Tube Station – he didn't notice the name – and quickly bought a day pass. The group ahead didn't bother, just vaulting the barriers and hurling abuse at the station staff.

They boarded a Northern Line train. He got in to a carriage two behind them and stood in the doorway so as to watch their exit.

In the pocket of his leather jacket he felt the handle of a bowie knife. It had saved his bacon a number of times, both in the UK and back at home in Syria. He'd taught himself to use it: he'd discovered that fast ruthless action normally won the day. Working the odd shift as a bouncer had taught him how to look after himself.

He had no real plan, but he suspected he would need to use the steel blade again that day.

*

They left the train at Waterloo Station, heading up multiple escalators to ground level. A sign board claiming cleaning was in progress at the female toilet was kicked over, a poster for the army ripped off a wall.

"Keep it calm in here," Jeremy told them as they came to the main line station. Too many normal and Transport Police to be making trouble.   .

They plodded relatively quietly through the station, reverting to their boisterous selves once out on the roads again. They didn't look back, people kept out of their way, and the sun still shone down. The ten minute train trip meant they were a little more sober, but that wouldn't last for too long. The next boozer was just around the corner.

*

Jasim trailed behind and watched them enter the Grey Horse Public House. The landlords name – Sanjay Singh – was displayed above the door, and he hoped that the man was out and that his staff were not all Indians.

He noticed that the big guy with the short blond hair seemed to be the group's leader. Whatever he said seemed to be adhered to, and whenever a bottle was handed around, he was always offered the first swig. He'd also been the one who had hit the speaker with the loud-hailer. He was therefore marked as target number one.

Lighting a cigarette in a shop doorway opposite the pub, he settled down to wait for the next move.

*

It was ten o'clock at night, and Jeremy and the gang had now been to eleven different pubs. People were dropping off from the crowd as their alcohol levels got the better of them, heading off to squats and apartments to sleep it off. The hard core element kept at it, catching another Tube to a rough part of Southwark that they called home, back to their own pub.

The Devil's Dog had never been a nice bar, even when first built. Now it was more than rough: A boarded up window let little light in to the place, and the front door had been kicked off so many times that the owner had finally replaced it with a steel one. The pebbles from the pebble-dashed front were mainly knocked off from people kicking the walls and hitting then with poorly parked cars, and the green paint on the door and window frames was almost totally gone, leaving the cheap rusted metal under it exposed to the elements.

"Hey Jez, who you with tonight?" a drunk girl in a short denim skirt yelled. "I'll fuck yer if yer'll buy me a few beers."

"Piss off Kate, yer not even thirteen yet. Prefer to fuck yer mother."

"I'm still the best shag around here," she told him, pushing up to him. "Give it a try."

He shoved her away.

"Give me a London Pride Mick," he told the barman. "And a whisky chaser."

"You got money?"

"These wankers will pay you. I just gave them an afternoon out, so pay-back time."

His buddies laughed and got their orders in, someone chucking a couple of tenners on to the bar.

"Got this from the barman you laid out earlier."

"Money's money," the barman conceded.

A girl of about twenty came from the back room. She was pretty in a strange sort of way, her long black hair pulled back in to a severe ponytail. She was wearing a pair of black leggings that ended mid-calf, and a loose T-shirt knotted at the waist. Across the front in large letters was the word GUESS.

"Still about 36C," Jeremy said. "Come here and let me have a feel."

"Piss off," she told him.

"Hard to bloody please you Siobhan. Never bloody happy."

She flashed a fake smile and went to the beer pump to help serve, ignoring the men.

"I'll have you one day," Jeremy said. She just kept serving.

"Let's have a game of pool Jez," Chopper said. "We can worry about sex later."

"Sex is never a worry. Just who it's with."

*

Jasim didn't feel safe in the neighbourhood. It was rough, he didn't see any people of his own kind, just white guys with skinhead cuts and a group of black youths who appeared to be selling drugs. If he hung around here too long he'd get some hassle, of that he was sure.

Should he just leave it? The guy had too many friends in the bar with him, so going in there was a total no-no. Hanging around out here was too.

He walked past the pub, noting an alley at the rear where some large wheelie bins were parked. He looked to see if anyone was watching him and seeing no-one moved quickly in to the rubbish area. A closed door led on to it from the bar. The outside light that should have illuminated the area had been smashed sometime in the past, leaving the area dark and full of deep shadows.

Parking himself on an upturned beer case, he decided to give it an hour.

*

"Another beer Jez?"

"And a whisky mate. Anybody got any fags? I'm out."

They'd played two games of pool that had taken about forty-five minutes because they were too drunk to concentrate, and now were lining up on the dart board. The group was down to six people now, plus Kate, Siobhan and the barman.

It was just gone eleven and the bar staff wanted to go home but knew better than to try and get the boys to leave. They hung around at the bar, watching a black-and-white telly in the corner. Kate hovered around the men, getting the odd drink and seeing who she would stay with that night.

Jeremy was finding it hard to think, his eyes getting heavy. He'd been drinking about eleven hours on and off, and sleep would catch him soon.

"Last game," he told the others.

"I'll get a last beer for us," Chopper told him.

"Right."

Siobhan looked across to the darts area, noting the guys were about finished. "Time to start the clean-up," she told the barman. "You get the glasses done then head off home."

"Are you OK to lock up with these guys?"

"I grew up here, so I know how to handle them."

She poured two final pints as Chopper approached the bar, appearing to read his mind, not realizing that the beer was making him speak too loud. He dropped a fiver on the bar and took the drinks away, sipping from his glass.

"That's me done."

"Then get on your way. I'll lock up."

Even in his semi-drunken state, Jeremy noted the exit of the barman and the fact that only Kate, Siobhan, Chopper and himself remained.

Was this his lucky night?

*

Outside in the trash area Jasim was getting cold and a little worried. No-one had seen him, or at least no-one had been over to see what he was playing at. A large brown rat had shocked him when it had sprinted from behind the wheelies towards the open road, probably hiding in the shadows since his appearance there.

He'd been there about an hour, and it really was time to move on.

Just then the barman walked past the entry to the alley, head down and on a mission to get somewhere, probably away from the area and in to his home. They must be closing, he decided.

He stood up from the bottle case, his left knee clicking audibly in the quiet of the alley. Standing on his right leg, he shook out the left, getting the circulation running again. He bent down and rubbed both knees with his hands, partly to assist in their wake-up process, and partly to warm himself. Hands to his mouth, he breathed hard in to them, feeling the warmth from his lungs.

"I'll wait until they go," he whispered to himself.

The danger here was leaving with any of the gang that was left. In their inebriated condition, an outsider would be a good excuse for a fight, and the odds may be far against him.

He moved behind the wheelie bins where he could watch.

*

Chopper had finished his beer.

"You ready Jez?"

Jeremy looked at the bar where Siobhan was tidying some bottles. "Not quite," he replied.

Chopper followed his gaze and nodded. "I think I'll give Katie here a try. She thinks she can teach me a thing or two, so why not?" He winked at the drunk teenager.

Jeremy shook his head. Sex was great, but sex with a minor was just too risky. "Enjoy," he told Chopper.

The ex-Angel was on his feet, hauling Kate on to hers. "Come on then princess," he said. "Show your daddy what you got." Her skirt had ridden up her skinny legs revealing a rather a pair of greyish knickers that had once been white.

Jeremy looked to the bar, where Siobhan was gathering the rubbish bags together. "Night Kate, night Chopper. Don't do nothing I wouldn't do." Chopper shot him a lewd grin.

They headed for the door.

Jeremy turned as the back door slammed shut. Siobhan going out with the rubbish. Time to move.

*

Jasim ducked behind the bins when he heard the release bar on the door squeak. The row of four bins hid him well, so he wasn't too concerned, and even less so once he saw between the bins that it was just a young woman, her hands full of plastic bin bags. He heard rather than saw other people passing the alley, a man's voice and woman's giggle.

It appeared the night was over.

The girl put the bags down next to one of the bins then lifted the lid. One by one she dropped the bags inside the wheelie.

Just then the hinges on the door groaned again, light flooding out.

"Thought I'd come and give yer a hand Siobhan," a drunken voice boomed out. It was a voice he recognized from earlier: the ringleader.

"I'm doing fine Jez, so get off home."

The light faded as the door closed, and he heard the man belch and then move toward his hideout.

"Come on Siobhan, give us a chance," he told the girl. "A bit of fun never killed anybody."

"I said go home Jez."

He was up to her now, she still putting the bags in to the bin, him behind her. Jasim guessed he put his arms around her and she swore at him. "Piss off Jez!"

*

Jeremy wasn't listening now. He was acting on beer-fuelled lust, his hands circling the girl's waist and pulling her towards him.

"You know yer want me," he whispered, his lips close to her ear. "Let's do it inside. We can lock the front door."

She was struggling but was no match for the big guy. His left hand moved upwards, grabbing a handful of breast. She stamped downwards with her right foot, scrapping down his shin and smashing in to the top of his foot.

"Bitch!" he screamed, arms around her waist, picking her off the ground. "You fucking bitch!"

168

He started to carry her towards the pub door, her arms trapped but legs still kicking at him.

"Let me go, you bastard!"

*

Jasim slipped out from behind the bins, his bowie knife already in his hand. This guy in front of him was a real piece of work, and it was time for him to get his comeuppance. He moved silently and quickly up to the struggling couple, deciding how to best use the situation. Because of the beer and the fighting girl, the gang leader noticed nothing.

Time was running in slow-motion, but the distances were small and Jasim was up to the man in a second. In one move he grabbed the guy's head from behind and pulled it back, exposing the throat.

"What the fuck..."

These were the last words Jeremy managed. The knife hand was guiding the blade over the unprotected throat, slicing it open. Blood flooded out, pouring down the man's chest and the back of the girl. Jasim felt the blade hit bone, knew that the job was done. He let go of the body and it slipped to the ground, still holding the girl and taking her down too.

He ran from the alley.

*

Siobhan rolled away from the dead Jeremy, tears rolling down her face and gasping for air. Her knees were scraped and her back was wet and warm: she knew it was his blood.

Pushing herself on to her hands and knees, she looked at the dead man, the dark shiny gash under his chin, and then at the back of a figure running from the alley. She had no clue who it was: Jeremy had plenty of friends, but also plenty of enemies.

Pulling herself up the wall and on to her feet, she walked back in to the pub and called the police.

Printed in Great Britain
by Amazon